I0537834

SEX SHOT SERIES

VOLUME ONE

Cover Design and Layout: We Read Literary Services
Published by: Wickedly Erotic Press
A Verb Publishing Company

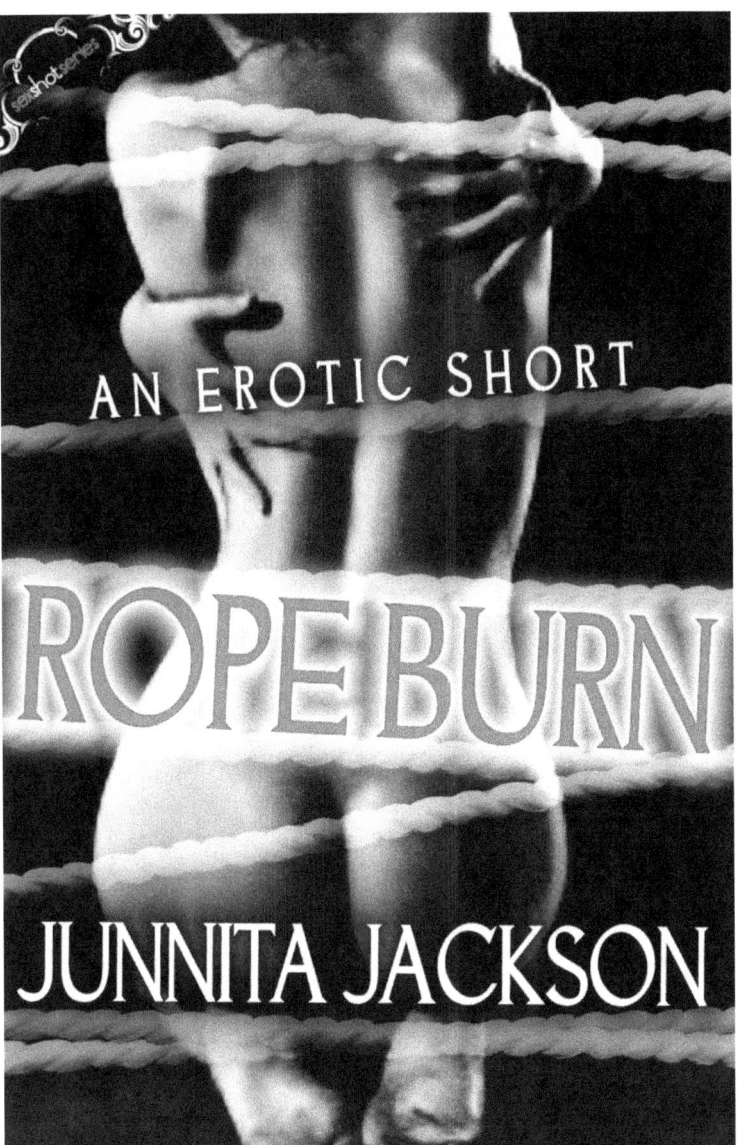

AN EROTIC SHORT

ROPE BURN

JUNNITA JACKSON

ROPE BURN

Diane looked at the invitation again for the 3rd time tonight.

It's has to be a mistake. She thought to herself. She turned the smooth cream envelope over again to see her name printed clearly on the front in red ink. The envelope held no clues as to where it came from. It was simply...there. She had opened the door to her apartment and there it was, lying on the beige carpet next to the fresh coffee stain she'd made this morning trying to juggle too many things on the way out the door to work. Diane placed the envelope on the coffee table in front of her; she removed her shoes and rubbed the soles of her feet. She hated her job at the pizza shop. She only had it to make ends meet; everybody knew teachers didn't make a lot of money. Two jobs five days a week, she was exhausted. She didn't have many friends so she knew no one would be inviting her to anything.

Diane leaned forward and carefully slid the invitation off the table. It was so beautiful in its simplicity. Crème colored paper with red gilded lettering. Even the wording on the invitation was simplistically beautiful:

Where: Delila's Bakery
When: Tonight after 11pm

Why: Why Not?

Delila's Bakery? Diane knew just where that was, Delila's Bakery catered the schools teachers meetings; but why were they open so late? She pondered this as she rose from the couch and made her way to the bathroom. Diane pulled her shirt over her head and dropped it into the hamper against the wall. She turned to stare at her reflection as she leaned on to the sink. She knew she desperately needed to update her look but she wasn't sure how. Diane studied her fail-safe hair style. Micro braids from the African braiding shop on Fulton Street, to the best of her knowledge these braids were *always* in style. She studied her eyebrows; she had tried to arch them herself by following a YouTube tutorial but the results were less than desirable. She was still trying to grow them back. Her skin was okay, not great just okay. She was cute. That about summed up her beauty. Cute. Ordinary. Even the way she dressed was ordinary. Diane didn't have any type of personal style and she knew it. She often copied looks from magazines or fashion blogs but she still didn't seem to pull it off quite right. She sighed and stepped out of her pants and panties and turned on the water in the tub. She turned back to the sink and stared at her body. She had nice full breast and full hips. She had a pudgy midsection but by no means could she be called fat, she just wasn't toned. She liked the way her breast looked in this bra. It was one of those Victoria Secret water bras. She reached around her back and undid her hooks. Diane stepped into the tub and turned the water off. It was hot just like she liked it. The steam quickly fogged up the window.

Diane laid her head on the edge of the tub and tried to relax. The image of the invitation kept appearing in her mind's eye.

Delila's Bakery? Open at 11pm...

It was beginning to intrigue her. It wasn't like she had anything else to do. Diane reached for her sponge. It was a vibrating sponge she bought from a toy party she went to over a year ago. And quite frankly this was the only action she'd had in about that much time. She flipped the switch and smiled as it came to life in her hands. Diane closed her eyes and plunged the ball below the surface of the water and aimed straight for her pleasure spot. She let the visions of a buffet of men ravaging her body take over. She was the main course in a smorgasbord orgy. Diane lay on top of a wooden picnic table covered in pineapple pieces, strawberry slices, grapes, mango pieces and other various pieces of fruit and whipped topping. Men of all sizes and colors dined on her using their fingers and tongues to lick and lap up their dessert. The heat from her skin caused the whipped topping to melt and drip trails down her breast, between her legs and to even pool in her belly button. No spot on her body went unattended.

Diane's body shuddered with an intense orgasm.

The water in the tub splashed onto the bathroom floor.

Diane loved her Battery Operated Boyfriend but sometimes he was too efficient. Her moment of pleasure felt...well...like a *moment*. She'd always tell herself next time she'll tease herself, or next time she'll use batteries from the dollar store so the vibration isn't as intense. But in her mind she knew that would just frustrate her. Diane used her thumb to switch the sponge into the off position. She closed her eyes and thought about lying down for a few minutes. She didn't know what time it was but her apartment building was starting to quiet down. She couldn't hear loud music, or children running back and forth above her head. She finished washing her body and climbed out of the tub.

In her bedroom the clock read 10:12pm. Diane picked up the phone and called information for the number to the bakery. She allowed an automatic connection to the bakery. The phone just rang, after a while a message came on giving the hours of operation and this week's specials but making no mention of any extended hours or special events happening tonight. Somewhere in the back of her mind she had made the decision to go. Like the invite said...Why not?

Diane went to her closet and sighed heavily before opening the doors, she knew she wouldn't find anything of any real appeal in there. She figured she would keep it simple with a black pencil skirt, a white button down blouse, and a pair of black pumps. Diane wasn't sure what the evening held so she was pleased that she should be able to fit into any casual situation with this outfit.

She took her time dressing, and pinning up her hair. When it was all said and done and she was all powdered and primed, Diane grabbed the invitation, her keys and her purse and walked out of her apartment. It was a few minutes after 11pm but she wasn't far from the bakery. Her mind raced with *what if* scenarios the entire trip to the bakery. Finally she stood in front of it.

Delila's Bakery.

It was closed.

The lights were out and there was no sense of life inside at all. Diane looked at the invitation again. This was the correct place. She walked around the side of the building and heard laughter as a door opened and closed in the distance. Diane walked slowly towards it. When she reached the door she tried to open it and it was locked. She rang the bell beside the door.

The door was opened by a tall woman with legs for days.

"Yes?" the woman inquired.

"I... ummm...have an invitation. I'm not sure if I'm in the right place."

"I'm not sure you are in the right place either." She stated looking me up and down. "May I see your invitation?"

Diane gave her the invite she studied it a moment and smiled. "A newbie, huh? This should be interesting." She chuckled.

"Could you tell me what type of function this is?" I asked

The leggy woman at the door stepped forward and unbuttoned the top 3 buttons on my blouse. I tried to button them back and she slapped my hand away. She stepped back and let her eyes roam over me, studying me. She reached around and pulled the banana clip from her hair. The tiny braids fell all around Diane's face and shoulders.

"Shake your head like this." The leggy woman tossed her head from side to side then flipped her hair to the back. Diane copied the gesture. "Now take those stockings off."

"Go bare legged?" Diane asked.

Who does that? Diane thought as she slipped out her shoes and removed her coffee colored stockings. She balled them up and stuck them in her purse before putting her shoes back on.

"You're ready." She said handing me back my invitation. "Take your invitation to the baker and order something on the menu. Because this is your first time out and you received a newbie invitation the 1st menu item is on us. Any additional item you order will be at least $300 for a small portion."

"$300 for pastry?"

"As I was saying..."The leggy woman continued, ignoring Diane's question. "We do accept all major credit cards and of course cash. If you pay by credit card it will appear on your statement simply as Dessert. Please keep an open mind and you will be awarded with unimaginable pleasure." With that the leggy woman directed Diane towards the menu board at the back of the bakery.

Delila's Bakery was filled with the aroma of vanilla, cinnamon, honey and...was that cannabis? Diane took in the sight around her. She had never seen so many fishnet wrapped legs wear such high heels in her life. The women wearing the fishnet stockings also wore aprons and well... not much else. They each carried a tray of strawberries and assorted glasses of champagne. One stopped in front of me with a brilliant smile and asked if I would like something from her tray. Her nipples were very visible under her apron and for a moment I was at a loss for words. She repeated her question and I nodded yes while opening my purse. My hand shook.

"First time here, huh?"

"Yes." I admitted nervously.

"Well, let me give you a quick intro on how things work around here. The items on the trays are complimentary. That includes the strawberries, alcoholic beverages, condoms, lubes...just about anything being passed around on the trays. If you have special preferences you can request them but understand they will cost you a pretty penny. The menu behind you will give you an idea of what goes on behind that door," She said pointing to a set of double doors being guarded over by 2 deep chocolate men without shirts on. "Now you don't have to order anything, you could kind of stay in this area and mingle with the crowd and maybe order something later with someone that may interest you out here. There is no room for judging anyone here and tonight you can be whoever or whatever you desire. We don't use names here, you are completely anonymous. How did you come across the bakery? You don't seem like our regular clientele, if you don't mind me asking."

"I got an invitation stuffed under my door."

"Red lettering?" Diane nodded. "Okay, then you pretty much can order anything on the menu for free... at least one item... I say pick something you wouldn't normally do and enjoy. Someone paid a pretty penny to send this invite."

"Can you tell me who?

"It's anonymous, but someone thought you needed a good time."

Diane picked a strawberry up by the stem and bit into it. A stream of liquid slid down her chin. Her eyes grew wide and then closed in pleasure as she licked the liquid off her chin.

"Amaretto. Here have some champagne." And with that the leggy woman walked away.

Amaretto soaked strawberries. How divine.

Diane took another bite.

Diane took in her surroundings as she sipped from her glass. There were men and women everywhere. They openly flirted with one another and occasionally paired up at the menu board before disappearing behind the double doors together.

Diane made her way over to the menu board and was taken aback by all the choices. The list of possibilities made

8

her wet. Or was it the champagne? Either way she could feel her inhibitions lowering. She read the menu carefully; each dessert sounding better than the one before it.

Strawberry Shortcake- Lather yourself in whipped cream and strawberries and be the dessert of choice. This dish feeds 4.

Creamy Cinnamon Twists - Be submissive to this dish. This dish of creamy cinnamon twist feeds 2.

Diane decided she would choose one of these dishes. The Strawberry Shortcake reminded her of her usual masturbation daydream and wondered what it would be like in real life. But the mystery of the creamy cinnamon Twist was calling to her.

Be submissive.

Diane couldn't help but to be drawn to the many possibilities that could bring. That was it she decided. Creamy Cinnamon Twist it was. Diane walked across the room and put her empty glass and strawberry stem on a tray of a passing waitress and grabbed another of both off her tray. She handed her invitation to the baker at the counter and gave her order.

"Will you be participating or just watching?" the baker asked. Diane hadn't considered the possibility of just watching, she assumed she would be participating. But she was such a voyeur. She often sat in bed at night watching her neighbors through the window.

"Um. I guess I'd like to watch." It sounded almost sinful to her ears.

"OK, if at any time you'd like to participate, just press the blue button on the wall." The baker instructed as he gave her a slip of paper and a cinnamon twist. "Give the paper to the man at the double door."

"Thank you."

Diane walked to the double door and handed the shirtless man the slip of paper. The overwhelming urge to lick his bare chest was a surprising feeling. Maybe it was the liquor. Diane followed the instructions she was given and her senses were assaulted with the smell of sex and fruit and something sweet she couldn't quite put her finger on. Her ears were assaulted with the sounds of moaning, dirty talk, skin slapping skin and what sounded like someone getting a spanking. She smiled to herself and wondered briefly as to who introduced her to this new world. Finally she was at her destination.

Diane took a deep breath and opened the door in front of her. On the other side of the door the room was decorated with restraints; ropes, chains, and muzzles. She couldn't believe her eyes, straight ahead the room was separated by a huge glass. She sat in a chair in front of the glass and watched as a woman was strapped into what looked like a dentist chair. She was blond and round and completely naked. Her hands were bound above her head and her feet were bound together, crossed at the ankles. Her eyes followed the two men she was with around the room. They finally came to stand in front of her and began to slowly undress. Shirts, jeans and shoes became just a heap on the floor.

Diane twisted in her seat. The strange scene in front of her excited her. She couldn't wait to see what happens next. Between her legs throbbed, she needed some type of stimulation, she wished she had her sponge. A moan from the other side of the glass redirected Diane's attention. The men stood on opposite sides of the woman and masturbated. Diane watched as their hands slid up and down their own dicks. She twisted in her seat again. The strokes began to get more aggressive.

Up and down.

She watched as they spit on their hands and went back to stroking themselves. Nobody touched the naked woman strapped to the chair. Diane wondered why she was even there. Then she listened as the woman barked out directions on how they were to stroke themselves. The woman instructed one man to stand close to her face and for each stroke to brush her lightly on the cheek.

Diane closed her eyes and twisted in her seat again, how she wished she had her sponge. It would be such a welcome treat right now. She opens her eyes to see the 2nd man in the room rubbing his dick on the bottom of the woman's feet. The woman's body shook with what appeared to be an orgasm. She told the man jerking off on her cheek to stroke faster, harder and to giver what she wanted. Diane stood and wiggled out of her wet panties. She wondered if anyone else would enter the room she was in, or if it was just one person at a time in here. Her attention went back to the glass when she heard what she thought was a door close. She was right; a woman had entered the room. She wore only a sapphire blue thong and heels to match. She giggled at the scene in front of her and drank the rest of the champagne in her glass before setting it down.

"Can I join?" Her request was approved with a simple nod from the woman strapped to the chair. Sapphire shoes sauntered to the bottom of the chair and watched as the man continued to rub his dick on the soles of the round woman's feet. Diane wanted to join the party but was a bit reluctant. She wondered if she would be received well. The woman in the Sapphire shoes was gorgeous. She had a small waist and ample hips, her skin looked to be the same color of the cinnamon twist Diane held in her hands. Sapphire shoes breast were swelled like a new mothers, and the only hair she had on her body was above her shoulders.

Diane stood and began pacing the room. She walked towards the blue button on the wall, then back to her seat. She repeated this twice more before hitting the blue button. She decided she still wanted to watch but she also wanted to experience it with all her senses. She wanted to hear clearly, to see clearly, to smell it all. She just wasn't ready for the touch or taste yet. A door opened off to the side room. Diane hesitated before walking toward the door. The sounds got louder as she neared the door. There was a very short walk down a corridor before she found herself in the room where all the action was. They barely acknowledged her presence; she stood off to the sides taking in everything. She also noticed she was the only one in the room fully dressed.

Diane watched as the Sapphire woman took the other woman's toes into her mouth. She paid careful attention to each toe, allowing her tongue to encircle each one before her mouth closed over it. The man at the foot of the chair continued to stroke himself while simultaneously allowing the head of his dick to stroke the soles of her feet. Diane notice the man's stance wasn't as steady as a few moments ago. He was about to cum on her feet. She had to get a better view. She could feel her thighs slide together as she walked towards the end of the chair. She was so fucking wet.

A guttural moan filled the room as the man at the foot of the chair came. His head was thrown back in pleasure as he continued to stroke himself. His strokes were coming slower now but he was still cumming and the girl sucking the toes was lapping it all up off the woman's feet. It was also on her cheek and she made no move to remove it, she just continued to give attention to the woman's toes.

Diane moved away from that scene when she noticed the woman in the chair looking at her.

"You can't be in here and not participate."

"Oh, I'm just watching."

"Watchers are for the other side of the glass, suga. Come here." The woman on the chair summoned.

Diane walked over to the woman but kept her eyes on the man that was jerking off near the woman's face. The woman told Diane to bring her something in the room that interested her. Diane walked around the room taking her time and observing. Another couple walked into the room kissing and touching and made their way to a set of pillows in the corner. Diane looked back at the lady in the chair and noticed she had already forgotten about her. She focused her attention back to the couple in the corner. He was fucking her doggy style. It has been since forever since she was fucked like that; raw emotion. He was basically manhandling her. She seemed to love it as he grabbed at her hair and pulled to get in deeper. Diane's scalp tingled at the thought of her braids being pulled. She noticed her hand was to her breast and she was slightly pinching her nipples through her shirt and bra.

The woman tried to wiggle away from the man's grip, but he held tight. Diane cringed at the thought of him about to break her tiny frame. She could barely be seen under him. His body covered her's almost completely as he bent into her frame. She cried out in pain and he sighed releasing her. That was the moment he noticed Diane. He sized up her thick frame and smiled. His smiled called to her and she found herself moving towards him. Her fingers worked on their own undoing the rest of the buttons on her white blouse. She caught a light breeze as her blouse left her body and floated to the floor. She moved toward him and

13

took the place of the woman that was there just seconds ago. Diane waited patiently as the man change the rubber he had on for a fresh one. Safe sex hadn't even crossed her mind. She just had this unexpectedly overwhelming urge to get fucked. No kissing or gentle petting. No, she just wanted straight fucking.

Diane was on all fours in front of this crayon brown stranger who wore only a jet black rubber. The head of his dick was huge, but the rest of it was average. Average length, average width, but the size of his arms and the toned cuts on his chest and stomach told her he had power behind each stroke. And, after all that was what really matter right? Diane knew there would be no feeling him all up in her stomach but she had no doubt this would be a great ride. She inhaled sharply as the electricity from his touch sent sparks through her. He was sliding the palms of his hands up the back of her thighs as he lifted her skirt up and let it gather at the waist. Diane felt the tops of his thighs brushed up the bottom of hers as he nestled into her. She waited for the pain she knew she would feel when he entered her. It had been so long since the last time.

The pain struck but the pleasure quickly followed as he entered her. He was digging his thumbs into her waist as he grabbed her and rocked her body back and forth.

He stopped; for just a moment and she could feel him reaching for something. She hung her head to catch her breath and to use her pussy muscles to pull him further into her. She felt him reach under her, touching her belly with something rough. She felt herself being jerked back into his body. He had wrapped something around her body to give himself more leverage to manhandle her. She secretly wished he would have chosen to pull her hair instead of to wrap this rope around her waist. The burning sensation of

14

the rope and the pleasure of each stroke were too much for her to bear. Stroke after stroke Diane was brought closer and closer to something she had never felt before. This man she was allowing to manhandle her was riding her like a bull in a rodeo. He pulled the reins with each stroke and she cried out in pleasure at each stroke even though her belly ached. The sweat rolling off of him onto her back made her wish they were in the shower instead of in a room filled with who knows how many other sex acts going on.

Diane felt his stroke slow, but he had not loosed the grip on the reins. She could feel him gather the rope in one hand and with the other he stuck his thumb in her ass. She exploded with an intense orgasm. She no longer had control over her body as it bucked under him, feeling her orgasm he grabbed the reins tighter and fucked her harder. Pumped furiously into her, until he exploded inside of her, not wanting to waste a single moment of pleasure he continued to stroke her forcefully until his dick went soft and slid out of her pussy on its own.

He collapsed on her; their bodies curved together, her knees hurting and her belly on fire. He still had quite a grip on the rope wrapped around her belly, until she started to wiggle underneath him to signal to him she was ready to get up. He loosed his grip and she attempted to stand on weak legs.

Diane gathered her belongings and went in search of a bathroom. She found one on the far side of the room and opened the door. She ignored the couple fucking against the wall and entered into the stall to relieve and dress herself. She went to the sink when she was done and washed her hands. She looked at her reflection in the mirror and smiled a naughty smile at herself. Burning sensations under her blouse cause her to lift it to look at her belly. There were

15

several lines on raw red whelps where the skin was just gone; rubbed away. She couldn't believe what she was seeing. She took a few pieces of paper towels and stuck them to her belly until she could tend to it properly when she got home. Diane walked through the bakery dazed, as she looked for an exit. She pushed open the door when she found it.

The street outside the bakery buzzed with its normal morning activities. Diane looked at her watched and she discovered she only had about 45 minutes before she was to start teaching her first class. Where had the time gone? She'd have to go straight to the school. She would have to freshen up in the school bathroom.

Exhausted and sore Diane made her way to her classroom where she taught English.

Maybe I'll just give a quiet reading exercise. She thought to herself. Diane turned the knob to open the door and reached into the dark to caress the wall in search of the light switch. The bright light caused her to squint and shield her eyes. She could feel a headache coming on and remembered she had some aspirin in her desk drawer. Diane hung her coat on the rack near the door and slowly made her way to her desk while gently rubbing her temples. As she reached her desk she noticed a white box with a hot pink bow. Diane looked around the room before reaching for the box.

A present? For me? She thought, secretly hoping it was another invitation to Delila's Bakery.

Diane lifted the lid off the box and peered inside. She was shocked to see her name printed on a small card as it was on the envelope. Diane picked up the card and flipped it over. There was nothing printed on the reverse side. She looked up when she heard the bell ring and the children running through the hall to class to begin their day. Diane turned her attention back to the box on the desk in front of her. She adored the tissue paper. It was a hot pink just like the bow, and it looked so fragile. No one had ever given her such a nicely wrapped present before. She wanted to savor the feeling but the kids were taking their seats in her classroom. She could wait until she had a quiet moment to herself to finish opening it. Diane looked at her watch, contemplating. Her next free moment won't be for several hours.

As Diane pulled back the tissue paper she gasps and her hand flew to her mouth to hide her wide grin. Inside was a tube of A&D Ointment, and an after-hours menu for Delila's Bakery. Written on the bottom of the menu was a simple note.

This should help with the rope burns.

The End

Her Wish

Eva woke from a fitful sleep. Her almond honey skin flushed crimson from her nightmare. Next to her, her lover Lux slept soundly. Eva was secretly envious of how easily she made getting and staying asleep seem. With no hope of getting back to sleep, Eva headed downstairs for some midnight reading and hot green tea.

Lux reached into the blackness for the reassurance of her lover's presence. She was alone. She shivered against the cool sheets in the spot that should have been Eva's. Lux sat up in the bed groggily, knowing instinctively what had happen and where she would find her.

Another sleepless night.

Eva knew without worry that the gentle steps coming from down the hall belonged to Lux. A flurry of butterflies swarmed her stomach. Lux took a seat at the opposite end of the chaise lounge Eva was resting on. Her big brown eyes traveled Eva's figure lovingly. Underneath her old discolored t-shirt, Eva's skin glistened invitingly. Her beautiful c-cup breast rose and fell with each breath. A slim waist gave way to full thick thighs and a rounded ass. Eva swears it the southern cooking she grew up on and 200 squats daily that's to blame for her figure. Lux took Eva's newly pedicured feet into her cinnamon brown hands and massaged it while she held Eva in her gaze.

"I think the green tea, is helping to keep you up. Why don't you drink the chamomile I bought you?"

"It's nasty."

Eva laid her book against her breast.

"I'm sure Stephen King isn't helping you sleep." Lux removed the book from Eva's chest and laid it open on its pages next to the forgotten cup of tea. Eva moaned softly as her life partner worked the tension from her. Lux looked ravishing in a cream and red lace camisole and short sleep set. The light colors against her deep cinnamon brown complexion were such an alluring sight that at first glance Eva was lost for words. Lux's puffy brown eyes displayed her exhaustion. Eva knew the only reason Lux had come was to ensure she was okay.

"I didn't mean to wake you," Eva said, her voice soft. Lux smiled adoringly.

"It's okay. I'd rather be awake with you, then sleeping without you in our bed." Lux's throaty alto voice sent a chill up Eva's back.

Eva sat up to face Lux. Her slate gray eyes caught Lux in their embrace. Lux could feel her temperature rising. Everything in her grew warm. She could feel Eva's heady gaze slip underneath her camisole and across her large brown nipples. Lux opened her arms to receive her lover. Eva crawled the length of Lux's brown body until their faces were inches from each other's. Eva sighed as Lux wrapped her in a sensual embrace. Lux tilted her head up to receive Eva's kiss. Their lips melted into each other. Lux's full lips parted to inhale Eva's tongue. She was struck by how something as simple as the taste of green tea that still lingered on Eva's lips, could send her pulsing.

21

Lux's breathing went shallow.

Their kiss deepened.

Lux spread her legs wider and was rewarded with the slow grind of Eva's pelvis against hers. She could feel her creamy pussy already growing moist with desire.

Eva inhaled the jasmine scent of Lux's skin. She felt her body surrendering to the cravings of the woman beneath her. Her pink nipples stiffened against the fabric of her t-shirt.

She heard herself moan softly as Lux grabbed her ass. The cotton fabric of her t-shirt offered little resistance against Lux's touches. Try as she might Eva couldn't think of one good reason why she would want it too. Eva's fevered kisses began to move to the long delicate column of Lux's neck. She could feel Lux's pulsing against her mouth as she sucked and licked the yielding flesh. Beneath her Lux moaned and writhed sensually. She put one hand in Eva's vibrant red head; the other stroked the smooth skin of her hip. The creamy flesh filled her palm uninterrupted. She loved how she always went to bed with no panties on. She could smell the heat rising from her center.

Eva burned a trail of kisses to the supple spilling of Lux's breast. With both hands occupied she pushed Lux's breast to the center of her chest and sucked her large brown nipples simultaneously. They quickly hardened. Eva sucked them hard and took turns nibbling one and then the other. She had to be careful not to bite too hard, but sometimes she couldn't control herself. Her mouth watered for the taste of Lux's skin. Eva pulled each delicious nipple into her mouth, her tongue swirling circles over Lux's brown buds. Both of them moaned and whimpered erotically. Their hips gyrated against each other's. Eva felt goose bumps forming against her skin. Her body flushed with passion. She loved the

22

sounds Lux made for her as she devoured her. Loved the way Lux's fingers tangled in her hair as Lux clenched and unclenched her fist.

Their desire building, Eva released her grasp just long enough to request they return to bed. Lux's nodded lustily as she took Eva's hand and guided her towards their bedroom.

Once in the bedroom Eva discarded her t-shirt. Lux followed suit carelessly removing her camisole and matching boy shorts. The crisp coolness of their haven did nothing to stifle the fire building between them. Lux strode to where her lover stood.

They kissed deeply, taking time to savor the feel of the others mouth and tongue. Lux suckled Eva's tongue. Eva nipped at Lux's lower lip. Lux's hand roamed freely across the wonderland of Eva's skin. She knew exactly how Eva liked to caressed and kissed. Eva's wish was Lux's pleasure.

She slid her fingers along Eva's high waist. A soft tremor of anticipation passed through Lux. Eva moaned her delight and gripped the soft rounds of Lux's plump ass. The silken feel of her lovers' curvaceous ass caused a heat wave through Eva's body.

Lux sat on the edge of the bed and pulled Eva into her embrace. Eva spaced her legs to straddle Lux's well-toned thighs. Her long lashes fluttered rapidly as Lux took one taunt pink nipple between her teeth. The sharp tings from Lux's pleasant bites rippled through Eva. Every movement became a carefully orchestrated dance of tongue and teeth. Lux could smell the scent of her lover's growing need and found herself greedy for the taste and feel of her.

Lux slipped two fingers between their bodies. She found the glistening flesh of milk and honey between Eva's legs and thumbed the engorged bud. Eva held tight to Lux's shoulders as she rocked back and forth against her hand, covering it with her sweet drippings. Her whimpering moans filled the air around them.

Lux slipped the fingers inside her lover. Eva nearly toppled over at the sensation. Lux curled her fingers and thrust against Eva's g-spot. Eva cried out in pleasure. She rocked violently against Lux's expert fingers. Lux continued her probing and sucking until Eva nearly collapsed in an orgasm. Eva's body convulsed. She babbled Lux's name in a gut wrenching stutter as her climax stole her words. Lux's body tensed. Eva always made the most exquisite sounds when she came.

Lux put her still dripping fingers to her lips. She drank the sweet nectar from her fingers and moaned deeply. Eva kissed Lux until she was breathless. With little resistance she pushed her to the bed. Lux's breast bounced in tiny circles. Eva knelt before Lux's open legs. Her moist flesh quivered as she blew hot breathes against it.

Lux squirmed and moaned and fondled her breast with one hand and reached for the top of Eva's head with the other. Eva planted herself soundly. With her mouth open, Eva kissed Lux's glazing pussy. She licked and sucked and sampled each inch of Lux's throbbing opening.

Her tongue dipped inside of Lux. It captured the creamy filling and Eva swallowed it willingly. Each sip of the cream made her more delirious than the last. Her mouth filled with the splendor of Lux's spilling. Eva tightened her grip on Lux's thighs as she delves deeper into her core. Her mouth watered for more and more. Lux arched her back under the onslaught of Eva's tongue. She whimpered and moaned. Purred and gnashed her head from one side to the other. Her mounting pleasure was uncontrollable. All she wanted was to explode into the hot mouth of the woman she'd spent the better part of the last three years with. Lux pushed Eva head deeper into her throbbing wet pussy. She ground her mound against Eva's mouth. Eva moaned and whimpered as she sucked harder. She tried to swallow Lux's clit. She wanted all that was being offered. Lux's orgasm was a powerful tsunami flooding Eva's hot mouth; her muscles spasm. Her eyes rolled behind her eyelids, her toes curled, fist clenched. Lux's body gave into its most primal desires and released.

For the rest of the night they traded orgasms. Each of them gorged themselves on the other. Until all there was left was sleep.

....

"I've been thinking about our anniversary," started Eva. Lux hardly looked up from the short story she was writing. She was use to Eva's antics and knew that any sentence that started with 'I've been thinking....' generally ended in trouble. Lux smiled dimly.

"And what have you been thinking sweetheart," she responded. Eva knew Lux was trying to humor her. At best, Lux would hear her out and then continue writing. Luckily, she had a plan.

"I was thinking, we could maybe invite someone to join us," Eva spoke softly, her voice dropping an octave for affect.

Lux stopped typing and looked up at Eva. Their eyes met. Neither budged under the others stare.

"So... for our anniversary you want to have a threesome?" Lux was not amused, although a few names of possible willing participants sprang to mind. Lux went back to typing and for a few minutes silence collected around them. "So who is this person?" asked Lux not once taking her eyes from her screen. There was no doubt in her mind that Eva had already picked someone.

"Ryan Joseph." Eva couldn't look at Lux as the name tumbled from between her lips. She'd laugh at the expression that she was sure Lux was wearing but knew better than to provoke Lux.

A penis?

Lux pushed the laptop from her lap. "Let me get this straight, for our anniversary you want us to have a threesome, with the pool boy?" The inflection in Lux's voice wavered. It wasn't that she'd never slept with men. Only that she'd given up men for women and hadn't thought twice about the decision.

"Just think about it babe," said Eva.

"I don't have to think about it. I don't want the threesome." responded Lux and with that, she went back to her story.

Eva left the room disappointed, but not defeated.

Later that night, Lux lay in bed waiting for Eva to come from the shower. She was getting dangerously sleepy and was on the verge of dozing off when she heard the bathroom door open. Eva had been unusually quiet since their conversation. Lux felt guilty. She wanted something special and memorable for their anniversary too, but had been thrown a loop with Eva's suggestion. Eva crawled into bed with her back to Lux. It was an act of frustration. A way of saying she was not interested in the rose scented perfume Lux had doused herself with. Nor was she moved by the sensual music playing in the background or the burning candles.

Lux reached out to touch her and Eva inched away just before contact. Lux pulled back her hand as though she had been burned. Her hurt feelings bled to disappointment and minutes later her own anger. It was unfair that Eva expected her to give so much, but promised so little. In her own show of defiance she turned her back to her, too and fell asleep.

A short time later, Lux tried to turn over in her sleep. Annoyance struck as she tried to reposition over and over. Finally she opened her eyes to find her hands tied with bondage rope to the bedposts. Her feet shared their fate. Alarm bells rang in her head until she caught sight of a smiling Eva sitting to the right of her.

"What are you up too?" she asked her lover half amused.

Eva's response was a cold, wet, tongue to Lux's right nipples. Shivers ran down Lux's spine. Her body tensed and released as Eva played and teased each breast. Eva held the ice in her mouth and sucked each nipple into hardness. Lux whimpered and moaned unprepared for the sensation and helpless to do anything about it.

Eva trailed the melting ice down Lux's stomach. She took her time, knowing the longer their foreplay the easier Lux would be to persuade. The ice melted against Lux's warm skin. She squirmed against the bed. She pulled at the rope hoping to get free, but it would not yield. Eva trailed even further down. She stopped at Lux's hips and took her time licking the pressure point there. Her tongue drew figure eights and hearts against Lux's sensitive inner thigh. Lux murmured her name. She pleaded with Eva to let her loose, to stop teasing her. Eva deafened to her cries and proceeded to indulging herself on Lux's cocoa body. When Lux was sufficiently enticed Eva reached for her other tools.

It wasn't until then that Lux notices the area of vibrators, clamps, powders and oils on the bed side table. First was the blindfold, then the candle wax. Eva slowly dribbled wax against Lux's chest. Lux winced and arched at the pleasurable pain. Each time a new spot, a new sensation coursing through her. Her blood boiled the buildup Eva was creating threatened to overtake her. The soft wax dried quickly against her skin. Eva soon moved on to something else. She dusted Lux's skin with a strawberry flavored powder.

Hungrily, Eva lapped up the powdered sugar from Lux's skin. Gone was the gentle lover of last night. Tonight Eva was famished and Lux was a feast. She would take her time to devour every part of Lux that she thought would fulfill her need, from the powder to a flavored stimulating nipple cream, then more of Eva greedy mouth.

Fingers.
Ears.
Neck.
Breast.
Hip.
Clit.
Knees.
Toes.
They all got their share of Eva's greedy mouth.

Lux thrashed about in their bed. Her mind spun wildly trying to grasp the sweet torture going on. Every bit of her tingled and she was sure she'd had a few mini orgasms while she waited for Eva's next attack on her senses. Eva reveled in the way Lux moaned and groaned at each turn. She knew it wasn't long before she'd be begging for relief. Eva kissed Lux's neatly trimmed pussy. Lux thrust her hips forward to Eva's waiting mouth. Eva tongued the creamy pussy and Lux wailed in unparalleled pleasure. Just as a heavy climax descended on Lux, Eva pulled back, leaving Lux gasping for air and aching. Eva repeated this cycle until Lux thought she would go mad with desire.

It was then she felt the pushing. The unfolding of her tight pussy as Eva pressed deep inside her pussy walls. Lux could not speak. She was suddenly mute as Eva pushed at least nine hard inches into her tight wet center. Eva found a rhythm. She prolonged the strokes as long as she could by pulling almost completely out then plunging back in again. Each time, Lux arched to receive her. Eva pushed deeper, harder; wanting desperately to feel Lux shake with unbridled passion.

Lux hadn't the slightest idea what to make of this. What type of trickery would cause her lover to tease her to the edge of oblivion and then deliver her to the beast? Still, she couldn't hide from the delicious frenzy her body was experiencing.

"You like this hard dick in your pussy baby?" Eva's voiced dripped with saccharine. If Lux were not blindfolded she would have surely succumbed to the seduction dancing in Eva's eyes. There was no escaping the truth.

"Yes baby, yes. I love that hard dick in my pussy…. Harder, please…" responded Lux. She could barely talk and breathe at the same time. Eva complied with one arm wrapped around Lux at the base of her back; she slammed the cock into Lux's velvety depths, creating tidal waves of orgasms as she did so. Eva was not immune to her lover's sultry cries. When Lux bucked wild beneath her she gave up her attempts to hold back. Her orgasms, a thousand sweet undoing's fled from her as if it had been imprisoned for a thousand years.

Before she collapsed completely…

"Say it…" she whispered against Lux's ear.

"Okay," responded Lux.

"Okay…What?" Eva probed further.

Lux's voice was barely above a whisper.

"Okay we can fuck Ryan."

....

A few weeks later on their anniversary, Lux and Eva was the perfect host. Dinner and desert were both beautifully filling and awkward. It had been pre-discussed what would happen. Ryan had agreed-even seeming excited. Now as they stood before him, he was unsure where to put his hands. Eva found herself frustrated at how he fumbled with her bra. She didn't like the way he kissed her either. Lux was the first to admit something was wrong.

"You know if you're a virgin. You can tell us. We promise to keep your secret." Her devilish smile instantly put Ryan at ease. His green eyes twinkled at her teasing. He chuckled and his curly black fluttered. "I'm sorry. I am being rather clumsy." Ryan responded, his gentle tenor voice, not at all what Lux expected. She opened her mouth to speak, but was interrupted by Eva.

"How about you pick one of us to start with, then the other can join in when you're more acquainted." Eva offered. Her voice infused with suggestion.

"I'd like that," Ryan returned, his gaze locked on to Lux.

He didn't notice her attention was on her lover who she was certain had just propositioned him. It wasn't until his mustache tickled the spot between her shoulder blades that she realized his decision. Eva's eyes widened briefly as she watched this man with her woman. Ryan wrapped his arms around Lux's waist. He slid them up slowly until he cup her breast in each hand. Lux drew in a sharp breath. It had been so long since she had a man to touch her this way, she'd forgotten what it was like to have the heavy hands pressed against her. She leaned her head back against Ryan's shoulder as he tasted a spot behind her ear. He nuzzled her thick wild hair and inhaled deeply her vanilla scent all the while pulling her body flush to his. Lux sat with her back to his chest between his legs. His shirt had been removed earlier in the night, as had her dress and Eva's blouse. His tanned skin glowed against her brown body as he kneaded her nipples between his fingers.

Lux moaned. She planted her hands on the strong muscular thighs on either side of her and leaned back further into his arms and closed her eyes. Ryan made his way to her neck and gave her open mouth kisses against the fine lines of it. He moaned as she rocked gently in his lap. His dick responded quickly to her subtle persuasion. While one hand remained on her breast, the other traveled to the lacy red panties she was still wearing. Ryan pushed back the hem of the romantic creation. Lux's eyes flew open; she searched for her lover's reassurance. Eva smiled gently and licked her lips. Lux returned the sentiment and spread her legs wider, giving Ryan better access.

Ryan flattened his palm against the fine hairs trimmed low leading into Lux's pussy. He enjoyed the textured feel of her hair, it heightened his awareness to her womanly essence. He proceeded down further until he found the tiny flower he knew would be the source of her pleasure.

"Mmmm, you feel so wet," he whispered in her ear, "and you smell, so sweet". His beautiful tanned face blushed at his find. Lux nodded weakly. She was far too taken with his long fingers massaging her clit to respond. She moaned with pleasure as he deepened his touch and inserted two fingers inside of her. Ryan swallowed hard. He found himself completely aroused and taken by the woman who now bounced softly against his fingers. He loved the sounds she made as he rubbed and penetrated her center. Lux could feel her orgasm building.

Eva watched quietly as Ryan toyed with the places she savored. If she were honest she'd admit she was jealous, that she didn't want him touching Lux in all the places she touched her. But one cannot say that, when she was the one who suggested. Instead, Eva reached across the bed to Lux's empty breast. Ryan didn't move. Lux moaned harder. Eva replaced her hand with her mouth. She alternated pressure, hardness, speed until she felt Lux's hand in her hair. Ryan felt his orgasm thickening. He was harder than he'd ever been as he watched Eva's pink tongue flicker against Lux's nipples.

Ryan pulled his fingers from Lux's panties and licked every drop of her nectar from his hands. Eva finished undressing herself and Lux did the same wiggling out of the panties sticky with her juices. Eva helped her out of them and promptly buried her mouth in Lux's chocolaty mound. Lux feed her hunger. Ryan sucked in a sharp breath as he looked on. He slid from his position behind Lux and she lay down softly against the bed. On the sidelines he finished undressing and watched as Eva lathered Lux's wet pussy with her mouth. Their moans blended together and Ryan could not stand idle. He spread Eva's legs slowly, until her pink blossom was revealed. As she positioned herself on her hands and knees in front of Lux, Ryan positioned himself behind her and began to eat her pussy. Ryan stuck his tongue deep inside Eva's wetness. She whimpered, but didn't move from her face down position. Ryan sucked harder and circled her core with his tongue. Eva rocked back against his mouth and shuddered into an explosive orgasm. She lifted her head briefly to breathe. Lux was not done and hastily repositioned Eva's head between her legs. Both women moaned and groaned with pleasure.

Ryan licked every drop of cum that squirted from Eva's pussy. Briefly he tongued the tight rim of her puckered asshole. Eva moaned louder and bounced back against his face. Another climax took her. Ryan's dick dripped pre cum. He stood at the edge of the bed. His large dick bobbed free. He was at minimum eight inches, thick, and pink with a smooth circumcised head.

Eva scooted up the bed until she was side by side with Lux. Ryan crawled into bed with them. He opened his mouth to Lux's pussy and probed gently. When he was happily saturated with the taste of her he lifted and kissed her lips. Tenderly, he brushed his mouth to hers. She returned his softness. Eva stroked his throbbing cock with one hand and licked his exposed nipples. Ryan moaned at the sensations traveling through him from all directions. Lux took his face in her hands. He opened his eyes to look at her. Her eyes were hood with passion.

"Ryan, I'd really like it if you fucked me now." She whispered in his mouth. His breathe caught in his throat, but he nodded in understanding. Eva sat back as Lux opened her legs to Ryan. He hovered over her and planted kisses along her eyelids, nose cheeks, jaw line. Her neck, he laced with attention as he quickly slid the condom on that Eva handed him. Ryan pushed into Lux's wetness. A groan traveled up his spine and out of his mouth as she welcomed him within her tight, wet walls. Lux locked her legs around his back and pulled him in deeper. Ryan nearly lost it as she thrust her hips up to receive him He began slowly, adjusting to the feel of her smooth slippery core. As his pace increased, Lux dug her nails into his back and matched each thrust. Her body submitted to his. He kissed her mouth again. Lux closed her eyes and enjoyed his attention.

Somewhere in the chaos of her body exploding she found Eva. Lux broke the kiss and looked to her lover. Eva couldn't hide her disenchantment. Lux would not let her regret this, their anniversary present. She pulled Eva to her. Slowly Eva lowered herself onto Lux's mouth. With Ryan's breathe in her hair, she rode Lux's tongue. Lux could hardly contain herself. Eva riding her face was sweet enough without the skillful stroking of a hard cock between her legs. The combination of the two was almost too decadent. She licked and nipped at Eva's pussy until her lover spilled in waves of orgasm. When finished, Eva kissed Lux's wet mouth and sixty-nined her body so she could lick Lux's click as Ryan thrust in and out of her.

The room echo with sounds of the threesome bringing each other to endless pleasures. Lux clenched Eva's ass as they rocked to heaven. She pressed Eva's pussy deep into her open mouth and allowed herself a full belly of Eva's sweet juices.

After a time, the two switched places with Eva on bottom. Both Lux and Ryan indulged Eva in the same attention she'd given. Eva could feel everything all over her and couldn't decide if she wanted it to end so she could explode into pretty colors or if she wanted it to go on forever. Ryan held back as long as he could. He'd never been so turned on in his life. There was no way he was going to be able to hold out much longer. When the final orgasm ravaged Eva's body he pulled from her warm cum filled embrace. Lux and Eva then took turns sucking his cock until he came in a cacophony of moans and grunts. There wasn't enough oxygen in the room for the three of them to breathe. So they settled for short burst of air between kisses.

Ryan settled to the left side of Lux and Eva to the right. Without much else, they all slipped into slumber, no doubt contemplating what fun day break could bring.

The End

the anerotic short

LIBRARIAN

JUNNITA JACKSON

He always kept his books for a full four days after the deadline. He always returned them the Friday after, usually right before closing when I am the only one here. I was expecting him any moment now.

"The Library is closing in fifteen minutes. Please make your final selections and bring them to the desk for checkout. Computers will begin shutting down in ten minutes, so be sure to save anything you may be working on in the meantime. Thank You." I made my usual announcement over the loudspeaker. A line began to form at the desk. People with books in hand lined up one behind the other ready to take their newest adventure home with them. I smiled at the people as the line grew longer, for as long as I could remember I had a love affair with books. Even today as an adult I am hardly ever without a book. I love the feel of the pages and smell of an old book. There is almost nothing as satisfying.

I glanced up at the clock then the door.

Any minute now.

I rubber stamped the new due date on the inside back cover of every book that crossed my desk.

This time would be different.

This time I would say more than "four books...four days late...fifteen cents per day per book...that will be..."

The door chime interrupted my thoughts. There he was in his entire chocolate splendor. He stood a good 5'11 and wore a dark blue single breasted suit. I watched as he strode through the door with the books tucked under his arm. His eyes met mine and sent a shiver through me. His confident stride caused me to stand taller and roll my shoulders back, sticking out my chest. He commanded the attention of everyone in the room.

"The library will be closing in eight minutes. Please make your final selections and bring them to the desk for checkout. Computers will begin their automatic shutdown in less than 3 minutes. Please begin to save anything you may be working on. Thank you." The library still had a few patrons but as I looked around they were all gathering their belongings and were either headed toward the exit or got in line behind the few others still waiting to be checked out.

I searched the room for him again and made eye contact with him near the dvd rental section. He appeared to be perusing the titles, but I knew he was just waiting to be last in line.

I tried my best not to let other people notice me checking him out. I wonder what he did for a living. He looked like he hadn't had a shave in a day or two, but even that 5 o'clock shadow didn't take away from the presence he commanded. I swallowed as I watched him walk to the far side of the library to pick a new selection of books. He was purposely trying to be the last one in here with me? The thought caused me to exhale softly while lost in thought.

"Um excuse me, miss? Did you hear me?"

"I'm sorry." I said being jolted back to the here and now. "Could you repeat yourself?"

"I said I'm going out of town and won't be able to return the book in time. I asked you if I could be given an extension now."

"Oh, unfortunately no, you would have to go online to the web address listed on your library card and extend your return date there. You can do it up to 5 days prior to the expected return date."

I stamped the return date in the back of the book and handed her the stack.

"The library is now closed. This is the last call for your final selection." My heart nearly leapt out of my chest while making that announcement. There were only a few teenagers hanging around, taking their time exiting.

"Goodnight, Miss Charlene." Some of the regulars called to me. I smiled and waved good night as I reached in my pocket to grab the keys to lock the door. I put the keys on the counter as I continued to check the final patrons out. I looked up and saw him at the end of the line.

Our eyes met and he smiled.

I didn't.

Why didn't I smile? Maybe he will think it was a shy turn away.

One more until we are face to face; I wish I could look in a mirror right now. I needed to make sure everything stayed in its proper place. I made it a point to wear this dress today. It was a black and white print wrap dress. It flattered my plus sized figure. The dress was low cut but appropriate for the job, the tie on the side defined my waist, and it hung loosely over my ample behind.

I stamped the last book and said goodnight. I looked around the library and noticed it was just me and him. I inhaled.

"Did you find everything ok?" I asked when I noticed he only had 2 books. He was 2 books short of his usual 4.

"I did have a difficult time finding a few titles." He said looking at me while he put his overdue books on the counter.

"Oh? What titles were those?" I asked holding his gaze. He handed me a piece of paper with 2 titles written on them. My temperature rose while I read the titles. "Does it have to be these specific titles? I'm not sure we have those titles but I can direct you to the section where it would be. Maybe another title will do if we don't have...I'm sorry we are closed." I stopped mid-sentence to advise a woman that walked in.

"I just wanted to return these and the drop off box outside is full."

"Ok, I'll take those." I said as I walked toward the door, keys in hand. I locked the door behind her and sat her books in the return box. "I can take you to the selection we have." I said turning my attention back to the counter where I thought he was still standing.

"Lead the way" He said in my ear. He was standing right behind me. His breath on my neck made me want to poke my ass out to see just how close he was.

"As you wish," I said as I resisted the urge to poke my ass out, and instead put one foot in front of the other.

"Is it that simple?" He asked.

I stopped and turned to face him.

"Is what that simple?"

"Is my wish your command?" His eyes twinkled with mischief.

"Why Mr. Hill are you flirting with me?" I asked while turning in the direction of the row of books we would be entering.

"It depends."

"On?"

"If you are receptive to it." He said while stepping up behind me and putting his hands on my shoulders. He slowly let his hands glide down my arms, stopping at my elbow. I turned to face him, my back inches from the shelves of books. He didn't move. He stayed in my personal space, invading it...seductively.

I stared at him, glad that I decided to wear heels today. I was face to face with him. He was ignoring me...or so it seemed. He dropped his hand from my arm and stepped closer into my personal space. Instinctively I stepped back pressing my back into the hundreds of books that lined the shelves behind me. I gasped when his chest brushed up against my breast lightly. He reached over my shoulder and pulled a book off the shelf. He flashed the title at me and then stepped back slightly.

"Ever try it?" He asked.

"Try what?" I asked trying to pull myself together. He flashed the book at me again. "Discovering the power of Pre-Orgasmic Sex? No, I don't believe I've ever had the pleasure of...ummm...pre-orgasmic sex."

He pulled another book from the shelf behind me, this time not bothering to step back. He smelled like honey.

Thick.

Sweet.

Honey.

I closed my eyes and inhaled him into me. My thighs slid against each other under my dress. My breathing deepened, becoming shallow. I lowered my eyes, thinking of my next move; wondering if I should even make a move.

"The complete idiot's guide to Tantric Sex; ever read it?" He asked.

"No." I barely managed to get the word out. He bought his lips down towards mine.

"It's all about...breathing." He said while exchanging breath for breath with me. His lips were but a whisper on mine. I tried to gently lick my lips, but my tongue brushed his bottom lip slightly. I heard him gasp, barely audible but it was there.

"Breathing..." I repeated. He moved away from me slightly and looked me in my eyes.

"That's what I've heard. It's all about breathing. Can I kiss you?" He asked.

"Where...ummm...I mean why...umm..huh?" I sounded like a complete idiot. He seemed slightly amused. He put the book back on the shelf and took my chin into his hand.

"Why not?"

"I barely know you." I managed to whisper.

"What would you like to know?" He asked kissing the corner of my mouth.

"Umm...married?"

"No, you?"

"No. Engaged?"

"No. You?"

"No. Are you seeing someone?"

"No. Not gay. Not involved. Not living with my mother. May I kiss you now?"

"ummm...." He leaned in to kiss me full on the lips. Not wanting to resist his kiss I allowed my body to melt into it. His kiss was soft and sensual, but... no tongue. He stopped and stepped away from me. I'm sure my crayon brown skin was now underlined with bright red. "Sure, you can kiss me." I said through a chuckle. He laughed and grabbed my hand.

"Come here."

I allowed myself to be led by him. I couldn't help but to wonder what was going on here. I often imagined ravishing him when he came into the library, but I had no clue he was attracted to me. He led me to the far side of the library where people sometimes sat in the overstuffed chairs in front of the window.

"Sit." He said. I frowned at the one word command as I raised an eyebrow at him. "Please, sit."

I sat down in the chair smoothing my dress under me. I crossed my legs. He sat on the window ledge directly in front of me. He grabbed the arms of the oversized chair and pulled it closer to him.

I gasped.

He smiled.

"I've been watching you for a while. You're beautiful." He said as he ran his finger slowly down my crossed leg. I watched him as he watched his finger curve over my knee, down my leg and over my ankles. He slipped my black patent leather shoe off. "These are nice." He stated carefully putting the shoe on the floor beside the chair. He put my foot in his lap and started telling me about his life. Where he grew up at, what he does for a living and why his books are always late back to the library. I didn't hear a word of it. I watched as his lips moved and thought about all the things they could be doing right now. My attention bounced back and forth from the slow deliberate strokes he gave my foot to the movement of his mouth. "You haven't heard a word I've said."

"True." I slipped my foot out of my other shoe and put that one in his lap as well.

He smiled and began to stroke the other foot. I closed my eyes and let my mind wander.

"Tell me about yourself."

"Hmmmm....that feels good." Was all I could seem to say. He chuckled and released my feet. I opened my eyes. He was getting ready to take off his suit jacket. "Don't."

He stopped. "Why not?"

I took my feet out of his lap and moved to the edge of the chair.

"It's silly..."

"No, tell me."

"I always told myself if I had a man that wore a suit and tie, that I would be the one to undress him. I think a man in a suit is sexy" I stood and pulled him up with me. "Something about running your hand over his chest and up towards his shoulders causing his jacket to fall from his body...well it just does something to me." His chest was hard and his shoulders well defined. His jacket hit the floor. His eyes stayed locked on mine, but I was looking at his tie.

"Something wrong?" He asked.

"No." I ran my hands up his chest, over the buttons on his shirt. I wrapped my hand around his tie and pulled him closer to me. "Just something about a man in a suit and tie..."

His lips found mine and he kissed me, gently at first. His hands circled my waist and he lifted me up onto the chair. I stood a bit taller than him now but that didn't seem to matter. His hands began to wander over my back and ass as he caressed me. His kiss trailed from my lips, down my neck until he met my shoulder bone. He paused and looked up at me. "What?"

"You smell like honey." I smiled because he did too. His hands traveled over my ass and down the back of my thighs until he was no longer caressing the fabric of my dress but bare flesh. His hand traveled back up my thighs until his flesh met lace. He kissed my chest as he allowed

45

his fingers to find the flesh under the lace. I exhaled, and shuddered when his finger slipped into my wetness. He slowly removed his finger and then stepped back. "Can I..."

"Yes." I whispered before he was able to get his question out.

He pulled at the bow I tied on the side of my wrap dress to keep it closed. The bow fell undone and the front flap of the dress fell away revealing a deep purple lace bra and panty set. He moaned his approval. His eyes stayed glued to my body as he pulled at his tie to loosen it. He undid the first two buttons on his shirt and pulled the shirt out of his pants. He looked hot even in this unkempt state. He slipped his tie over his head and let it fall to the floor on top of his suit jacket. I licked my lips in anticipation of another kiss. He bent and placed a kiss on my round belly. I was usually self-conscious about my figure but he surely didn't seem to mind. He moaned and gripped my hips. I could feel him licking my belly button and the sensations it caused nearly made me fall off the chair. He gripped me tighter. I grabbed the back of his head and resisted the urge to push him further south. He left a honey scented trail from my belly button to the top of my panty line. He paused, and then looked up at me as if asking for permission to continue. I nodded and he hooked his fingers under the lace at the legs and begun to slowly pull my panties down. He was careful to kiss and lick every spot that he uncovered. My eyes followed his movements as my panties passed my sweet spot and was pulled down over the tops of my thighs, then over my knees, and down my legs, his trail of kisses left my head swimming. I felt light headed as he guided me to lift my leg to take my panties from around my ankle. I looked down at him long enough to see him lick from my big toe over the top of foot and slowly make his way up to my center.

I should have shaved.

That thought quickly entered and left my mind as his tongue parted my lips. I exhaled loudly. It had been so long since someone made me feel like this. He grabbed my hips and rocked me back and forth onto his tongue. My wet clitoris pulsated with each stroke. My breathing deepened. His grip tightened. I grabbed his head and moaned as I came and became limp folding myself over his body. He continued to lick and rock me slowly. I tried to slow my breathing, but his every touch sent a chill and shot of electricity through me. Finally he stopped and moved himself away from my body, gently helping me down off the chair.

I stood looking at the reflection of myself in the huge window.

"Think anyone can see us?" I watched my reflection in the glass while my question hung in the air. The sight of my dress hanging off my shoulders with my lace bra exposed was beginning to turn me on. Purple was such a seductive color. I couldn't see outside because the glass was tinted and plus it was dark out by this time anyway. He turned to look out the window but didn't answer. Instead he led me to the over-sized chair I was just standing in and told me to "Please, sit." I smiled and sat down. He knelt in front of me and gently opened my legs by hanging my legs over either arm of the chair.

"Wanna play a game?" He asked rubbing the inside of my thighs.

"Maybe..."

"I'll ask you a question and you answer. Let's see how long you can fight another orgasm."

47

"Why would I want to fight it..."

"Okay let's see how quick I can make you cum, then."

"I'm not sure I'm up for answering any questions right now." I could feel my body temperature rising with the gentle rubbing from my thighs.

"Just relax. Where are you from?"

"Brooklyn."

"Brooklyn." He repeated as he used his finger to begin spelling it out circling my clitoris. "B-R-O-O..." his fingers drew each letter as he spoke it. I moaned. He continued to spell. "K-L-Y-N."

"Oh shit..."I moaned gripping the sides of the chair.

"You like that?"

"Fuck yeah...."

"F-U-C-K-Y-E-A-H."

"No fair..."

"All is fair in love and orgasms. Are you close to cumming?"

"Hmmmm..." I moaned trying not to answer. I could feel the wetness dripping down my pussy over my ass.

"H-M-M...how many m's are in that?" The vibrations from his amusement sent chills up my thigh. His finger continued to circle my clitoris while he waited for an answer. "Are you going to answer?"

"Fuck no I'm not going t-..."

"F-U-C-K-N-O-I-apostrophe-M-N-O-T..."

"Ahhhhhhh" An orgasm ripped through me causing me to lose my breath. I grabbed him by the collar and pulled him closer to me. My lips to his, I kissed him. My tongue on his, I tasted him. My body convulsed as he pressed his finger into me and kissed me back. The beat of his heart danced against my breast. I wanted him to fuck me. NOW.

His lips disconnected form mine as he broke off our kiss. Before I could miss the warmth from his mouth he dipped his head to lure a nipple in his mouth through the lace. My body screamed. He needed to enter me, now! Reluctantly I broke our embrace and stood. I turned my let my ass brush up against him slightly while allowing my dress to hit the floor. I bent over holding on the arms of the chair and spreading my legs. When he didn't approach I swayed my hips from side to side to entice him. Still...no advancement.

"Need instructions?" I asked.

"No, I'd like an invitation. I don't go anywhere I'm not sure I'm wanted."

He was serious. He wanted to be invited in to...me. Here I stood, ass hiked up in the air and streams of cum rolling down my leg and he wanted a verbal invitation as if this position wasn't screaming fuck me. Fine.

"I invite you to put a condom on and enter me." My words, laced with seduction, lured him into action.

"Invite accepted." The sound of his voice caressed my spine. He reached into his wallet and pulled out a rubber. He released himself from his pants and my eyes followed his movements as he slipped the condom on. His movements seemed to be in slow motion as I tried to keep my anticipation in check. "How would you like it?" He asked stroking himself while letting his pants fall to the floor.

"Hard. Fast. And Now!"

He grabbed my waist with one hand and guided himself inside with the other. He slid in easy enough; I was so wet. Once he was in and we were skin to skin he grabbed my waist with his other hand. I felt him slide deep into me and pull out slow. This was not what I asked for. Did he not know the meaning of hard or fast? As if reading my mind his strokes increases, his grip became tighter. I gripped the sides of the chair and bit my lips as each stroke brought me closer and closer to another orgasm. He slowed his pace and grunted as he resisted the urge to cum. Stroke after stroke I could feel his body begin to shake as he slammed into me. His hands moved from my hips to my breast. He squeezed and stroked. I moaned as I felt my body give way to another intense orgasm. I shuddered under him as he wrapped his body around mine and bit me on my shoulder. His stroke slowed as he neared his orgasm.

"No, don't stop!" I yelled. "Faster! Harder! Cum for me!"

The top of his thighs made my ass and thighs ripple as he pounded into me. His grip on me was tight, his stroke strong and steady. His sweat rolled off of him and onto me, his honey scent getting stronger. Thicker.

"Oh, shit!" He yelled as he came. His knees buckled and he tried hard to continue to strong as he came. His strokes slowed and he pulled out slowly. "Damn, that shit was good!"

We both collapsed on the floor of the library and started laughing. "So, was that pre-orgasmic sex?" I asked.

"I have no idea, but would love to do it again."

"You have an open invitation." I assured him. And with that, the library had extended hours several times a week.

The End

aneroticshort

TASTE TESTER
JUNNITA JACKSON

Taste Testers

Annabelle Waters sat at her desk and went through the pile of unpaid bills again. Who knew she would have bills even in college. She should have stayed in the dorms like her parents wanted her to, but, no she had to exert her independence. After all 19 meant you were grown and ready to do whatever the hell you want to whenever you want, right?

Annabelle opened her laptop and logged onto Craigslist to see if the few items she had to sell had any interest. None.

Might as well browse the help wanted section. After several minutes she came across an ad for a Quality Control Taste Tester. "I can do this." She stated to no one in particular as she wrote the information down on a notepad and circled it with an orange highlighter. Annabelle continued to look through the help wanted before grabbing her cell phone, praying it still had service and dialing the number. She agreed on a time to be interviewed later that day.

Annabelle hated being the only girl in her dorm without any spare pocket change. While the other girls partied and shopped, Annabelle studied. She was there on scholarship; it was the only way she would ever be able to afford the Ivy League college out in Pennsylvania. She'd worked hard in High School not to follow in her family's footsteps and had been the only one able to even consider a possible college education. But her hand me down rags and hand sewn clothes had made it damn near impossible to experience the complete college experience. She was damn near invisible. Her roommate was one of the few people on campus that would even acknowledge her presence; they shared an apartment off campus.

Annabelle counted her little bit of change she collected in a jar and had just enough to catch the bus one way. She decided to walk there and take the bus back home after the interview. She freshened up and checked the time. It wasn't long before she needed to be there. She stepped outside and the heat told her it may not be a good idea to walk there and show up at the interview funky. She needed this job in the worst way.

The bus dropped Annabelle off right in front of the address she wrote down. She checked the address again when she noticed the sign said After Moonlight Adult Novelties. Yup, according to what she wrote down this is the right place. She inhaled deeply as she realized her pockets and her morality were singing two different songs. Her strong religious upbringing had her pacing the street in front of the building her interview was to be held in. She believed in a higher power but her hormones sometimes gave her amnesia when she searched the internet for her masturbation fix.

It was just a job. Annabelle tried to convince herself. Although she was taught to follow the ways of the church she also knew she needed to work to survive. Annabelle took a deep breath and pulled on the heavy glass doors. After signing in at the front desk and telling the guard why she was there she rode the elevator up to the 10th floor and followed the directions to the office the interviews were being held in.

"Annabelle Waters?" The receptionist asked after she signed in and took a seat.

"Yes."

"This way please."

Annabelle followed the tall statuesque woman with the four inch neon blue stilettos to a room with a small window, a rotating fan and a few unmarked tubes of liquid. She handed me a clipboard with a pen attached. "You are at least 18 years old?" The receptionist asked as she popped her gum.

"Yes."

"ID?"

"Um.. yeah… here you go."

She checked the ID briefly and handed it back. "Ok, you have 7 different flavors there in front of you," she stated pointing to the test tubes on the start white table. "When you identify the flavor write your answers besides the line with the corresponding number. You have 5 minutes."

"What is this? In the tubes."

"As the top of the form says, you'll be taste testing lubricants."

"Lubricants?"

"Sex oils."

"Sex oils." Annabelle repeated to herself as she walked toward the table. She picked up the first plastic eyedropper and took a sample of the first liquid and rubbed it onto the back of her hand. Hesitantly she placed her tongue on the spot she'd just rubbed. The taste was familiar but she couldn't quite put her finger on it. She repeated the process, this time not rubbing it in as much. The taste reminded her of applesauce so beside the first line she wrote Apple.

She repeated the same steps six more times with guesses ranging from single flavors to a mix of some flavors that tasted like one thing with an after taste of another thing, like Kiwi Strawberry.

This isn't so bad, Annabelle thought as she took her paper back to the receptionist. *I can certainly do this.*

"Thank you." The receptionist compared Annabelle's answers to the answer key taped to her desk. "Looks like you got them all right except two. You mixed them up. Those citrus flavors can be kind of tricky."

"Oh, okay, well thanks anyway." Disappointed Annabelle gathered her things and headed towards the door.

"Annabelle?"

"Yes?"

"You changed your mind about the job? You got enough right to start tonight if you were still interested?"

"Really? Hell yea, I want the job." Annabelle could barely contain her excitement. She thought for sure she would have to start the search all over again for a job. "And I can start tonight if you want me too."

"Great!. Read this and sign and initial where indicated on the last page. We can get you into a testing room in about an hour." Checking something on her calendar, the receptionist continued. "Tonight we are testing nipple and penis creams."

"Here you go." Annabelle signed and initialed where indicated on the last page and handed the stack of papers back.

Eyebrow raised the receptionist asked, "You read this before signing?"

"Yup." Annabelle lied, eager to get started. The receptionist chuckled, shook her head and accepted the papers she was being handed. She went over the pay fee and the schedule for the project. Annabel knew she would have a difficult time keeping up with the middle of the night schedule they gave her along with trying to get to class on time and stay awake. But right now her choices were very limited and she managed to convince herself this was a temporary assignment.

Annabelle was shown her working station by one of the other girls working there. It's set-up was simple, a work desk, a stack of papers, some baby wipes, something called a palate cleanser and a basket of products for testing. A note on a sticky pad stated today's products are nipple cream and dick sucking creams and underneath that were three flavors listed: Cinnamon, Cherry and Lollipop..

Annabelle went through the basket examining each of the bottles and tubes. The receptionist told her it was a three hour shift and for the life of her she couldn't figure out how to the draw the little basket of goodies out to three hours. Maybe it was the paperwork that took a long time. Annabelle picked up one of the papers in the stack and figured it can't be that, there were only five questions on there and they were multiple choices.

She sat down and picked up a jar of nipple cream that was simply marked: Nipple Cream - Lollipop. Annabelle screwed off the top and stuck her pinky finger on top of the whipped concoction. It reminded her of the whipped frosting her mom used to make from scratch when she was a little girl. She stuck her pinky in her mouth and scrunched up her nose at the taste. Annabelle grabbed a pen and paper off the stack and began to fill out the paper.

"What are you doing?" One of the girls startled her with the question.

"I'm starting my shift."

"Honey, did you read your contract?"

"Not really, I just signed it so I could get started." Annabelle admitted.

The girl looked at Annabelle amused. She had short brown hair that made her blue eyes really pop. Her skin was a beige color that made it hard to determine her ethnicity and the piercing on her lips made her appear a bit rebellious.

"Hey, T. She didn't read the "fine print." The girl laughed as she drew attention to Annabelle. "Honey, you should have read the fine print. We don't test these products out of their containers."

"We don't? Then how are they tested...umm"

"Call me Rox." She said when she realized Annabel didn't know her name. Rox pulled a folded up piece of paper out of her back pocket and read "Testing MUST be done on test subjects."

"Ok, where are the test subjects?"

"There." Grinning Rox points behind a glass panel at a line of men and women in robes. "These are the test subjects. Rox doubles over in laughter at the look on Annabelle's face. She loved messing with the newbies. College kids looking to get a quick check really got on her nerves. This was how she made her living, how she kept food on the table. But it also amused her because that was how she started. She was so young and inexperienced at life.

Rox studied Annabelle "You'll be alright. What we do is pull an assignment from the box. How many you do a night will determine how much you get paid. Your job is to taste the products according to the directions, anything extra you do is totally up to you and not required for the job to pay you. No matter what your tester says. Do you understand?"

Annabelle looked confused for a moment before she said she understood. But she wondered if she really did. She watched as the other employees picked an assignment out the box and then went into a locked room with a tester.

She was next. Her assignment read.

Assignment: Very Cherry Nipple Cream, Lollipop
Dick Cream
Test Subject: Male

Annabelle took a deep breath and went to pick out her test subject. She couldn't believe all these men and women were here to be licked on. She wondered if they were volunteers or employees and if this was some sort of rotation where eventually she would be the one in the line with a robe on.

Rox gave Annabelle a little nudge forward towards the line and told her she'll be fine. "You pick male or female?"

"Male." Annabelle answered, holding up the slip of paper for Rox to see. Rox whispered in her ear to choose the third one in the line and that she won't be disappointed. Annabelle escorted the dark skinned male to a room that simply had a lazy boy recliner, a desk, stool and a chair. It was all rather sterile...except the lazy boy recliner seemed out of place. She put all of her supplies and a clipboard on the desk and turned to introduce herself to her test subject and nearly bit her tongue when she saw him standing there naked. Annabelle looked for the robe he just had on and saw it hanging neatly on a hook beside the door.

"Oh, you're...naked and I'm Annabelle." She chuckled trying to avert her eyes from his hanging member.

"Yeah, I'm Calvin." He offered his hand to shake and the warmth of his palm sent a shiver over her.

"Ok, let's get started." She pulled her hand from his and turned toward the desk. Exhaling she picked up the nipple cream and tried to steady her shaking hands before walking over to him. "This is supposed to be a type of cherry flavor." Unscrewing the top, Annabelle brought the product to her nose and sniffed. Scrunching her nose she remarked it smelled like cough syrup. She stuck her finger in the jar and wiped it on his nipple. She tried not to notice the fact that his nipple felt like diamonds under her fingertip. Avoiding eye contact, she asked Calvin if it was cold.

"A little, but it usually warms up after you put your mouth on it." Calvin flashed Annabelle a million dollar smile and caught her off guard. He appeared to enjoy being a tester very much. Was he some sort of pervert? Or was she? No, she was doing it to pay her bills. That was all. Annabelle leaned forward to lick his nipple when she felt him grab the back of her head. "Don't be shy now. It's just a nipple. Plus you've got to suck on it to get the full experience of the flavor."

Annabelle pushed away. "I would appreciate it if you didn't touch me."

"But you can touch me?" He grinned, teasing.

"Well, I have to…" She Answered not quite getting it was a joke.

"Relax, I'm just playing. I like to give the newbies a hard time. And it's rare you would find a virgin in this day and age, let alone this business."

"I'm not a…virgin." Annabel tried to fill her statement with defiance, but the look on Calvin's face told her she hadn't hit the mark. "Can we just go back to work so I can go on to the next person?"

"I see you're uncomfortable. How about you take off your shirt and I can test this out on you." He reached for her shirt and tugged. The little buttons on her shirt came undone. She looked at him and laughed when his look turned from excitement to disappointment. Annabel stood there with her short sleeve button down shirt more than half undone but underneath was a men's white t-shirt. "Now, see, that's just not right. A rocking little body like yours should have a nice bra and panty set on. Not this."

"Can we just get back to it? She sighed.

"Ok, you tasted the first one. You need to fill out that form and get started on the next one." He said using his hard on to gesture toward the table.

"Thanks." Annabelle answered. She wasn't looking forward to this next product. She had never sucked a dick in her life. Truth be told this was the first time she had even seen a man in the buff up close and personal. Her body tingled and her face went flush. She wanted to take him all in, to just study his body. But she knew she couldn't do that without having exposed herself as being a virgin. With her back to him, Annabelle closed her eyes and tried to construct him from memory. She didn't think she would like a man with hair on his chest but the baby fine hairs drew a path to his penis. She had never seen one in person that wasn't on a baby whose diaper she was changing and she was getting ready to put this one in her mouth. Annabelle listened to her roommates talk about sucking dick and some of them loved it and some of them hated it, but the thing she remembered the most from both sides of the coin was No Teeth. She opened her eyes and turned to find Calvin using a baby wipe to get the cream off his nipples. Annabelle snuck a peek at Calvin's penis and wondered why a grown man didn't have any pubic hair. She found it rather odd. "Okay, let's do this last one so we can finish up."

"Your wish is my command." Calvin said as he took a giant step that placed him right in front of Annabelle. She hadn't even gotten out of her seat. "It may be more comfortable for you if you remained seated." Calvin put his hands on his hips and let his rock hard penis find its way towards Annabelle's mouth.

"OMG, can you please back up. Damn, I'm the one conducting the testing not you and your damn penis. Can you get it out of my face?"

"How are you going to put it in your mouth if it's not in your face?"

"You are enjoying this a little too much, and I haven't even started yet." Annabelle rested her hands on her thighs to try to draw attention away from the fact that she was shaking. She had a penis in her face and really all she could think about was *I wonder how it taste*. She tried to convince herself it was okay, if she enjoyed her work. You are supposed to enjoy what you do to make a living. Plus nobody knew her here and she was hundreds of miles away from any judging eyes back home.

"I tell you what, Ana…"

"Annabelle. Don't shorten it."

"Ok, Annabelle. I tell you what. If you do me, then I'll do you."

"What?" The thought of Calvin putting his mouth on Annabelle made her squeeze her thighs together in an attempt to control the pulsating between her legs. "What do you mean you'll do me?"

"Whatever you do to me I will do to you. Or better yet how about, whatever I do to you, you do to me. I'll go first to put you at ease." With that statement Calvin kneeled in front of Annabelle and began to remove her shoes. She was glad she chose to put her canvas sneakers in the wash yesterday, because those shoes can sure hold an odor. "I'm going to have to remove you pants, Annabelle. Stand up."

Annabelle stood, reminding herself that she should love her job. She stood still while letting Calvin undo her button on her jeans and she didn't move when Calvin shimmied her jeans over her hips. Annabelle stood in the middle of the room in her bare feet with her jeans pulled down around her ankles. She couldn't believe she was going to let a perfect stranger take her there, but here she was, lifting one foot after the other for him to slide her jeans completely off. Annabelle exhaled as Calvin traveled his hands back up her legs and rested on her hips. He hooked his fingers under the legs of her panties and began pulling them down. He inhaled her scent deeply.

"I can smell you." He said his voice low and almost inaudible.

"I showered." Annabelle stammered.

"Your heat. I can smell your heat." Calvin answered while bringing his face closer to her body. Calvin planted his face between her closed legs, holding her by the waist and inhaled. The gesture caused Annabelle to shiver. Calvin dipped his tongue between the folds of her lips and

Annabelle thought she was going to pass out. Sensing Annabel was unsteady on her feet; Calvin took the robe off the hook on the wall and laid it on top of the desk. "Sit up here" He instructed. Annabelle obliged.

Calvin parts her legs and slowly licks the outside of her pussy. Several slow strokes later he takes pleasure in her moans letting him know he is pleasing her. Annabelle wanted Calvin to believe she was experienced. She attempted to move her hips in tune to his strokes, but Calvin was holding her in place by her waist.

"Just relax and concentrate on what you're feeling." Calvin paused and looked up just long enough to convince her to let him be in control. Annabelle was suddenly aware of her awkwardness and tried to relax. Pleasure pulsed through her body. For every lick there was a shudder and a moan. She had finally settled into a natural rhythm all her own, gyrating her hips up toward his face. She kept grabbing the back of his head and just as quick as she did she would jerk her hands back as if she was touching hot coals. Calvin smiled and pulled her closer to him when he felt her shiver. Annabel tried to scoot her body back from him but Calvin held her tight, savoring the taste of her as she came in his mouth.

"I've never felt anything like that." Annabelle stated through her heavy breathing and then was immediately embarrassed at her inexperience. Calvin continued to let his tongue explore the creases and crevices of her pussy. He licked and sucked until she couldn't contain her desire or catch her breath. Annabelle fought hard against her pleasure to push Calvin away from her. With slanted eyes she looked at him, sitting there in there in that chair with his dick on swollen. She wasn't sure what to do with all these new sensations she felt. It never felt this good when she helped herself to an orgasm while surfing the internet for porn sites you didn't have to put your credit card information in to view.

Calvin stood and wrapped his hand around his dick. Annabelle looked at him wondering what he was about to do with it; then she remembered the second part of the testing. She twisted her body around to get to the basket behind her. Annabelle reached in and wrapped her hand around the toothpaste shaped tube of dick sucking cream and read the label out loud.

"Lollipop" She chuckled. "What kind of flavor is lollipop? Lollipops come in flavors."

"Taste it and see."

"Well, that is the plan, isn't it?"

"Well," Calvin held his dick toward her. "Let's get started."

Annabelle hopped off the desk and was suddenly aware of her bare bottom. She grabbed her panties and jeans off the floor and slid them back on. She took a deep breath and fixed her clothes before sitting in the chair Calvin just got out of. Calvin positioned himself in front of her, dick in hand. Annabelle opened the tube and squeezed a little onto the tip of her finger and then touched the tip of her finger to the tip of her tongue. Annabelle's expression said she approved of the flavor.

"You know that is not how you are supposed to do that?"

"Umm, really? How do you suggest I do it?"

With a wicked grin Calvin stepped closer to her and gently put his hand on the side of her face and guided it towards his dick. Annabelle wanted to push him away, but she knew it was part of the job and she needed the money.

Damn, the fine print. She thought, and then briefly wondered if she would have still taken the job even if she had read the fine print. There was a part of her that needed to know if she could make him feel like he made her feel only moments before. Annabelle moistened her lips and moved Calvin's hand from her head. "I can do it." She said very much sounding like a girl scout. She closed her eyes and tried to conjure up images of men getting their dick sucked from all the internet porn she's watched. She'd certainly seen enough of them to be confident in her skills to mimic what she'd seen.

Truth be told her dirty little secret was even though she watched more porn than what was probably healthy for a young girl. She was drawn to cartoons and midget porn. The idea of doing a search for cartoon midget porn caused a pulsating tremor between her thighs. Annabelle made a mental note to check that out later. She had never even touched a penis (except for a dildo in health class when she learned to put a condom on a guy) let alone put one in her mouth. Annabelle took her finger with the cream on it and wiped it on the tip of Calvin's dick. She leaned in to put his dick in her mouth and he stopped her.

"Rub it in." He told her. "Then put it in your mouth. Slowly."

She did what she was told. She slid his dick between her lips and looked up to see if she was doing it right.

"Watch your teeth." Annabelle pulled her head back until he was no longer in her mouth. She wiped her mouth with the back of her hand and asked exactly what that meant. How was she supposed to watch her teeth? "I don't know; just make sure you don't scrape my shit with your teeth. Cover them with your lips, I guess." Calvin had been on the receiving end of several blow jobs, but never really considered what happens after his dick disappears into their mouth. He just knew teeth were not a good thing.

Annabelle leaned in and reached for his dick. Previously she just let him guide his erection in her mouth but she figured she should at least touch it. She wrapped her hand around the shaft and was surprised at how hard and soft it felt at the same time, and the heat coming off of it made her mouth water. She leaned in, exhaled and let his dick penetrate her lips.

Calvin moaned at the warm moist feeling of the inside of her mouth. Annabelle slid her head back and forth so that his dick would glide in and out of her mouth. For a minute she forgot the purpose of sucking his dick was for her job and not for pleasure. Annabelle was surprised when she heard herself moan. She was enjoying herself. How could it possibly please her to please him? Was this the norm, or was she on some other level of special? Annabelle wasn't sure about what to do with her hand but she found that her lips kept slamming up against the side of her hand the faster and harder she worked on his dick. It occurred to her that this was more like stroking his dick with her lips than it was sucking his dick. She hadn't actually *sucked* his dick and wondered if that was what she was supposed to be doing. She figured it must be feeling good because every time she looked up he had his thrown back and his eyes were closed as he bit the corner of his lips. Still unsure of what to do with her hand, Annabelle squeezed as she caved her cheeks in around his dick and started to really suck on him. Calvin gasped and grabbed the back of her head, pulling her further onto his dick.

"Move your hand." He could barely get the words out as he used his other hand to grab both sides of her head and slide her back and forth over his dick. "Keep sucking."

Annabelle continued to cave her mouth in around his dick until her jaws hurt. She tried to pull back but Calvin had a tight grip on her head, and he seemed to be somewhere else lost in pleasure. She tapped him a couple of times on his hips and he looked down realizing she wanted to be let go of. He released her head, and she pulled back, massaging her jaws.

"Ow, why does it hurt?"

"It's a muscle like anything else." He said breathlessly. "Stick out your tongue like you are trying to touch your chin with it. Say ahhh, like at the doctors."

She looked at him skeptically before doing it. It actually seemed to relieve some of the pressure. She watched as he stroked himself to keep his hard on while she alternated between sticking out her tongue and massaging her jaws. Annabelle figured she could write her findings from the testing with the sucking she has already done, but him standing there stroking his dick in her face made her want to wrap her lips around it again.

She looked up into his erotically slanted eyes and read the question on his face as to whether she was going to finish or not. Annabelle reached out and grabbed a hold of his dick and slid it between her lips as she rolled her tongue around the head. She loved the taste of him, even though she could no longer taste the lollipop flavor she put on him earlier. Calvin moved her hand from his dick and put his hands on the side of her head to hold her steady. He slowly began to move his hips to fuck her mouth. He held he still while he moved his dick in and out of her mouth going deeper with each thrust. He was testing her gag reflex. When he felt the back of her throat and she still didn't choke or gag he picked up speed on his thrusting. Annabelle continued to roll her tongue around his dick and cave her cheeks in on him. She found herself grabbing the back of his thighs to pull him deeper into her mouth. She couldn't believe that her sucking on him made her feel powerful and in control.

"Oh shit!" Calvin rocked back on his heels, but held tight to her head. "I'm cumming."

Annabelle tightened her grip on the back of his thighs and continued to suck and stroke him with her tongue. She hadn't even taken into consideration as to whether she was going to spit or swallow, or what it would even feel like in her mouth. Calvin tilted Annabelle's head back and told her to let it just slide down her throat. That was the way he had always imagined it happened when he came in a woman's mouth, but Annabelle coughed and caused her teeth to lightly scrape his dick so he took his dick out her mouth while he was still cumming and a bit of it squirted on her cheek. She closed her eyes and opened her mouth as he continued to stroke out any extra juices he had left. Some landed on her eyelashes and more on her cheek. Annabelle often wondered what that would feel like when she watched porn at home. She liked it, she decided as she wiped her face with her hands.

Annabelle watched as Calvin picked up the robe from the desk and began to put it on. She looked at his limp dripping dick and wanted to clean him off with her tongue. Calvin slowly closed his robe while trying to maintain his balance. That was an intense nut. He fucking loved this job, he can get head and have no obligations after that and he got paid. He walked toward the door, stopping briefly to see what Annabelle was doing. She was looking at him like she was confused. She wondered if he thought they had made a connection and should she ask for his phone number. The look on his face didn't match up with her thoughts.

"Are you part time or full time?" He asked her.

Annabelle stared at him but didn't answer. His question reminded her that this was a job and now this assignment was over.

"Well I'm here most evenings if you want to use me as a tester again." And with that Calvin opened the door and exited the room.

Annabelle took a moment to get herself together, fill out the paperwork and ignore her feelings of rejection. "It's just a job." She said out loud to the empty room.

Annabelle opened the door, gathered her papers and backed out of the room turning off the light. Once the door was closed she turned to see a crowd of her co-workers standing staring at her. She started walking towards them to get back to her desk when she heard them start clapping. She was suddenly embarrassed and wanted to run and hide.

Rox walked up to Annabelle and threw her arm around her shoulder. "Don't worry honey; we've all done the walk of shame." Rox handed her the box to pick her next assignment. "The night is still young and there is money to be made."

Annabelle picked her assignment and sighed. She picked another dick sucking cream assignment. She opened her mouth and stuck out her tongue trying to touch her chin as she walked back to her desk before picking a tester. She alternated between that and massaging her jaw.

Can you get lock jaw from sucking dick? She wondered as she got back in line to pick an available tester.

The End.

BONUS MATERIAL

An Excerpt From:

one
Kat

My fiancé's face was buried deep between my legs. All I could think about was the eyeball staring back at me from behind my closet door. Dante had come home for lunch and little did I know on what he planned to feast. Little did he know I started a meal not long before he came home. How did I keep getting myself in shit like this? I guess I was just horny. Always had been. All the time. Must have been some kind of hormonal imbalance. It wasn't that Dante wasn't good at what he did because my baby could put it down. Like now, his fine ass was on his knees with his thumb in my ass and his tongue roaming from the crack of my ass to the swell of my clit. It just seemed the harder I came the more I wanted it. Shit, my motto was, I'll try anything once and would do it again just to make sure I didn't like it the first time. Just like air to breathe, I needed a hard dick to survive. I got my tubes tied 'cause I didn't want no babies. With my luck I'd have a girl and be worried that she would be a slut like her momma. Yeah, I said slut. I told y'all I need it so bad that even though I got my tubes tied I still went to my OB/GYN and got my Depro shot every three months so I wouldn't get my period. I wasn't gonna be laid up with cramps and blood. No way. Enough about that.

Dante had me on my back and was licking my ass, legs straight up in the air. See what I mean? He down there eatin' like it's Sunday dinner. I grabbed him by the back of his head, spread my legs wide and then wrapped them around his neck. I looked across the room and waved that big dick mutherfucker out of my closet. He stepped out licking his lips, dressed in one of my man's sweat suits. He stood there looking at me like he wanted to get on his knees and break bread with Dante. I pointed to the door and mouthed the words "get out". He leaned back in the closet and motioned for his friend to come on out too. His high yellow friend came out looking all upset because he didn't get a chance to get his dick wet. Oh well. I didn't like yellow men anyway but he sucked the hell out my toes.

"Cum for me, baby. I want to taste it."

"Right there...."

I grabbed the back of his head with two hands and realized I wasn't wearing my engagement ring.

"Oh shit!"

"You cumming for me, baby?"

"Uh... yeah."

"Come on then."

I arched my body back trying to get a hold of my ring off the nightstand. I grabbed it and slid it on my ring finger. Dante grabbed my ass and wiggled his stiff tongue in and out of my wet pussy and I unloaded right there in his mouth and all over his chin. He pushed himself up using his elbows and kissed me on my bare belly.

"Honey, I've got to get back to work. I wish I could stay." Dante looked down at his shirt and saw all the wetness I left behind. "Can you get me a clean shirt, babe?"

"Uh huh."

He went into the bathroom and I could hear the water running as I got up and went to the closet to pull out a clean dress shirt.

"You're going to be late," I yelled as I pulled back the mirrored closet doors. I chose a crisp white Sean John dress shirt from a hanger on his side of the closet. "Are you going to be able to grab something to eat on the way back to the office?" I asked, moving quickly away from the closet door. I just threw a pile of clothes from my lunchtime lovers on the closet floor. Dante made his way out the bathroom towel drying his face wearing nothing but his slacks and a smile. I held the shirt open while he grabbed a fresh T-shirt out the dresser drawer. He pulled the T-shirt over his head and tucked it into his pants. He grabbed me around the waist and kissed me on my neck.

"I already had something to eat." he said smiling slyly, swaying me in his arms from side to side.

"Go to work," I said, pointing at the clock on the wall.

"Oh shit. I gotta go, babe, love ya." He kissed me on my forehead and ran out the door while pulling his dress shirt on---

"Hold up, wait a minute. Wait just one minute. I don't believe this shit," Tamia said. She put her pizza down and swatted away a fly. We were sitting outside of a neighborhood pizza shop at one of their picnic tables. I looked her up and down and wondered why she always had something negative to say. Here I was trying to share my experiences with my girls and she always hated. She's been like this ever since we were in grade school together.

"Shut up and let her finish. I want to hear this." Vatyra said. That's my girl. She always had my back.

"I'm not tryin' to hear that. What about the pussy smell?"

"What?" Vatyra and I looked up at the bitch like she was crazy.

"The pussy smell. You're trying to tell me that he couldn't smell you sexing those other guys?"

Vatyra got up, walked towards the trash and emptied her tray. She set the tray on top of the trashcan, looked at me and shrugged her shoulders.

"Come on, Tamia, what's the problem?" Vatyra asked.

"I'm sayin' I don't understand her. She got this wonderful guy at home giving her everything and she playing hide the dick in the closet." Then the bitch gonna look at me and say, "I don't get you," like she was disgusted. "Not to mention the rock on your finger."

"What's to get? Why you trying to get me anyway? You supposed to be my girl. Yo for real don't judge me 'cause I damn sure don't judge you."

Tamia got up and made her way to the trash with her tray. She emptied the tray and walked toward my car that was parked near the corner. I got in on the drivers' side and Vatyra got in the back on the passenger side. Tamia stood with the passenger door open looking confused. I grabbed my sunglasses off the dash and put them on. I had to tighten up my make-up so I grabbed the rear view mirror and tilted it towards me. When I was satisfied with the image staring back at me I blew that sexy bitch a kiss. I started the car then realized Tamia still had the damn door open.

"You coming or what?"

"Did I bring a pocketbook?"

"Yeah you had that Coach bag I let you borrow six months ago." I looked in the back seat to see if the pocketbook was back there.

"Is it back there, Vatyra?"

"Naw, I think she left it at the picnic table."

"Check the table we sat at," I yelled out the open door. "That's why I don't like lending my shit out."

Tamia walked back towards the table. The pocketbook was still there; she grabbed it and turned to walk away. She opened the pocketbook to take out her sunglasses and dropped the damn thing, spilling shit everywhere.

"What?" she asked a man who stood in front of her, watching her pick up her stuff from the ground. She seemed slightly annoyed he didn't bother to help her. He just shook his head. Tamia sucked her teeth, finished gathering her stuff and stood to walk toward the car.

I beeped the horn for her to hurry her ass up. I didn't have all day to wait on her. Tamia looked over her sunglasses at me and slowed down on purpose. She was really trying my patience. Then, the same white guy stood in front of her blocking her path. I was sitting here waiting on Tamia and looking at her flirt with some guy who couldn't even help her pick up her shit off the ground.

"Look at her jungle fever having ass," I said to Vatyra, who was sitting in the back seat staring out the window. "Got the nerve to be judging me. Huh."

"Who's judging who now?"

"Shut up." I laughed.

I beeped the horn again to tell Tamia to hurry up. I managed to scare an old man crossing in front of my car in the process. I mouthed the word "sorry" to the old man and he gave me the finger. Ain't that some shit?

Tamia tried to move past the man but he stepped in her way. He was wearing casual Dockers and a clean pullover gray shirt. She tried again to move past him and he let her. She didn't look back but she made sure to put a little swing in her hips. She opened the door to the car and slid in with a motion fluid as liquid. She looked at Vatyra and me and smiled a sly smile.

I pulled off. "Slut."

"Right back at'cha." Tamia laughed.

Tamia looked out the window to see if her Caucasian admirer was still there. To her surprise his eyes were still following the moving car to the busy intersection. I weaved back and forth through traffic while we bounced to the beat of the latest 50 Cent song.

"I would fuck him," I said in between lyrics.

"Stop playin'. Who wouldn't?" Vatyra agreed.

"You mean who wouldn't she fuck?" Tamia added, smiling at me. I was not amused.

I continued to drive mouthing the words to the song and pulled up in front of a big brown building on the corner with the words COMMUNITY BANK perched high up on the roof. It was time to drop Tamia back off at work. She was supposed to take the day off with us but she couldn't afford to. She had to support her son since his father died. The whole situation was a mess. If you ask me I'd say she was still messed up over it.

81

"Thanks for lunch, Kat. Are we still on for tonight?" Tamia asked as she hopped out the passenger seat and Vatyra got in the front.

"You coming right?" I asked Vatyra. I didn't think I could deal with Tamia alone. She could be so uptight sometimes.

"Yeah, I guess, but we need to go to the mall so I can get something to wear and I need to get my nails done."

"I want to go to the mall."

"Tamia, you have to get to work. You should have taken the day off like we did. This was supposed to be a girls' day, you know spa, lunch, party, but you wanted to work."

"Not wanted, had to work," Tamia corrected.

"See ya, sweetie." I pulled off leaving Tamia standing on the sidewalk looking up at the building in despair.

"She left her bag again," Vatyra said as she picked the borrowed Coach bag up off the floor. I beeped the horn and put the car in reverse to meet Tamia. Vatyra's handed the Coach bag out the window to her.

"Pick you up at ten," I yelled out the window as I sped off.

To continue reading purchase a copy of If it Don't Hurt It Ain't Love.

An Excerpt From:

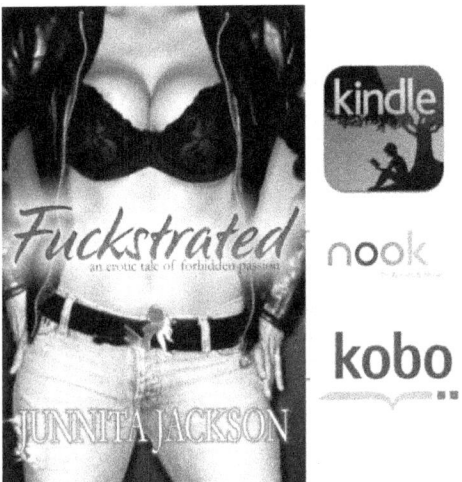

Friday

"Well, hello stranger." Victoria addressed her husband with a naughty grin. She was standing in the doorway of their spacious bathroom watching her husband adjust his tie. He looked up into the mirror to see her standing behind him wearing nothing but a pair of baby blue lace thongs and her wedding ring. He smiled at her as she sauntered toward him on the balls of her feet, how he loved this woman. Eric turned to face his wife, as she pressed her body to his and gave him a gentle kiss on the lips. "We don't have time for what you're thinking." She said as Eric ran his fingers down the side of her neck and over her shoulder.

"There is always time for lovin'" He responded, his voice laced with seduction.

"Mmmm, usually, but not tonight. You don't want to be late." Victoria purred while adjusting her husband's tie. "There will be plenty of time tonight, to celebrate any way you want." She stood on her tip-toes and kissed her husband. She ran her hand over his head and gripped the back of his neck as she slipped her tongue in his mouth. She pressed her body against his and gasped when he palmed her ass with both hands and pushed her up against the wall. Eric's kiss turned into a frenzy of fevered kisses trailing down her face and covering her throat. His thick lips were soft and knew exactly how she wanted to be kissed. Victoria's breathing became rapid and shallow. She looked down at her husband who was now circling his tongue around her left silver-dollar shaped nipple. His large chocolate hands gripped her pecan colored waist to stop her from squirming. Victoria began to protest but her sounds of "No" quickly turned into sounds of "Ohhhh" as Eric dipped his tongue into her belly button and tasted it. Victoria quickly relaxed into the fact they would be late to the awards dinner, that's if they made it at all. She grabbed the back of her husband's head and led him to where she really wanted him to be. He looked up at her and grinned as he loosened his tie and removed his jacket; both lay on the black marble floor they recently installed when they renovated the bathroom.

In the mirror behind Eric, Victoria watched his descent. He licked around her panty line before tracing the pattern of the lace with his tongue. She moaned, when he turned her to have her face the wall, still squatting in front of her. Eric palmed her bare ass and leaned in to kiss and nibble, when his cell phone rang. He paused. Victoria looked over her shoulder at him wondering if he was going to answer it or continued. Eric leaned in again, and the phone rang again.

"Just get it, it might be important." She said.

"See, this is how you can tell we are married, if we were dating, you'd be like 'fuck the phone'" He chuckled as he grabbed his jacket off the floor to get the phone. He looked to see who was calling, rolled his eyes and answered. "What Maurice?...Yeah, at the Plaza...No you can't go in jeans, it's a semi-formal event...Eventually, you are going to have to get some clothes other than the hood shit you wear all the time...what?...look I don't have time for this, pop still has some suits in the closet, pick one and put it on...yeah, whatever."

At the mention of Maurice's name, Victoria left the bathroom. She went and sat at her vanity in the bedroom and started to apply her makeup. Eric's brother Maurice was a mood killer for him, but he did something different for her. The thought of Maurice gave her goose bumps and made her nipples hard. She couldn't picture him in a suit, but she could picture him in his hood uniform of dark baggy jeans, a white tee, a fitted hat and some dark boots. Even in his baggy jeans she could see the imprint of his weapon of mass seduction. Victoria bit her bottom lip, took a deep breath and let it out slow as she loaded up her make-up brush with blush and skillfully brushed it over her cheekbones. She'd done her eyes before helping Eric with his tie earlier. She could hear her husband yelling into his cell phone that Maurice was a thug and needed to grow up. Victoria started to reach for a pretty pink shade of lipstick but changed her mind to match her mood and grabbed her Hourglass lipstick in Siren. This deep red color made her feel sexy and powerful. She pushed the thought of her husband's usual reaction to her red lips out her mind and let the vision of the ring of red this shade left on Maurice's dick flood in instead. Her pussy pulsed. She grabbed the remote to the stereo and switched it on. Trey Songz voice filled the room and she stood up from her vanity and slipped out of her baby blue thongs, she wanted to put on something that screamed scandalous. She swayed her hips to the music as she walked on the balls of her feet into her walk-in closet. After ruffling through her panty drawer she came out with a pair of bold red lace boy shorts and rose petal pasties covering her nipples.

She looked up as Eric came out of the bathroom looking annoyed as he returned his cell phone back to his jacket pocket. He looked at her and stared.

"Really, Vic, you're gonna wear the Devil's Red lips tonight? It makes you look cheap and turn that down." He pointed at the stereo.

"Funny, it makes me feel high priced." She countered. There weren't too many things she did that got under Eric's skin, but she felt like pushing all of his buttons today. She walked over to the stereo and turned it up a notch, and then she grabbed her pocketbook off the bed, pulled out a joint she had stashed in her purse and lit it.

"Really? I swear, lately I'm not sure who you are." He said when she took a pull from it and blew smoke into the air. Eric waved the smoke away and studied his wife. "What's wrong, Vic? Seriously, what's wrong?"

She thought about it for a moment before she answered. She wanted to tell him that he didn't take her *there* anymore. That his visions on what a wife should do in bed versus what a common whore would do was causing her to stray. She loved the way a hard dick felt in her mouth, she loved the power that came with a good head game. She wanted to tell him it was okay to be rough with her, to pull her hair and slap her ass, hell he could even choke her out if he wanted to. Victoria wanted him to understand that married people fucked, just as much or maybe even more than they made love. She wanted to be called his dirty whore, and she wanted to pick him up in a bar wearing a trashy outfit and FUCK him in a pay-by-the-hour no-tell-motel. Instead she said "Eric, we used to smoke weed all the time, remember? Remember we use to climb up on your mom's roof and get naked and fuck under the stars and smoke weed and drink that nasty ass St. Ides?" She walked towards him, her eyes begging him to remember when things weren't always so neat and tidy; when things were...fun.

"Not this again, Vic. We were different people then. There is a price that comes with success." He said backing away from the weed smoke. He didn't want it trapped in his clothes.

"Dammit, E, who gives a shit what we do in the privacy of our own damn home?"

"Get dressed. I'll meet you in the car in 5 minutes."

Victoria watched him leave the room, stepped out her panties, slipped into her ruby red strapless dress and shoes, grabbed her cell phone from her pocketbook and typed *I won't have any panties on tonight* and hit the send button. She dropped her cell phone into her evening bag and headed to the car.

The banquet hall at the Plaza was decorated in black and cream and was absolutely stunning. The servers were all dressed in white and circulated the room with silver trays filled with appetizers and tall flutes of champagne. The band played favorites from the 70's, 80's and 90's and Eric looked on as his colleagues danced with their significant others. Dinner had been served and the award recipients all had their five minutes of fame with their acceptance speeches. Dessert was now being served, a delicious sorbet with a mint leaf garnish. He looked across the table at his wife, brother and mother and smiled. The most important people in his life were here to see him awarded one of the most influential people in the health care industry, and he couldn't be happier, even with his wife giving him the cold shoulder since they got there. The band began to play again, now that the awards were all given out. Couples began to fill up the dance floor. Maybe a dance with his wife would smooth out some of the edges that got ruffled tonight. Maybe if he held her close and explained that all he is he owes to her love and support. He needed to make her understand that she was his everything and he hated when she was upset with him. Eric studied his wife as she was deep in conversation with a colleague of his, she was beautiful with her pecan complexion. He loved that she wore her hair pinned up to show off her long neck and sparkling earlobes. Eric could feel himself getting hard as he noticed how her earrings hung low and grazed her shimmery shoulders; just a few hours earlier he was lovingly kissing her there. She looked damn good, sitting over there with her clingy red dress with the long slit up the thigh. Victoria had purposely sat across from Eric instead of next to him to avoid having to speak to him. Eric turned to his mother and asked her if she'd care to dance.

Victoria watched as Eric whisked his mother off to the dance floor. She rolled her eyes and focused on the man with the bad hair piece she had been listening to for the past half hour or so, but, heaven help her she hadn't heard a word he said. She was more focused on what Maurice was doing up under her dress and praying her wetness wasn't leaving a big stain on her dress. She had been stroking him through his pants, but he pushed her hand away before she could bring him to orgasm. He didn't want to ruin the navy blue pin-striped suit he borrowed from his father's closet for tonight's event. He felt strange wearing a dead man's clothes even if it was the man he worshipped and idolized.

Victoria wanted to grab Maurice and disappear into the coat check room and finish what his brother started earlier. Maurice's finger circled Victoria's clitoris round and round and round until he could hear her breathing heavy, then he would stop. If she wasn't such a loud cummer he would go ahead and take her all the way there, but he was getting a kick out of watching the man she was talking to get turned on watching her breast rise and fall with her ever growing excitement. Maurice moved his hand from under her dress when he saw his brother approaching the table.

"Go dance with mama." Eric pointed in the direction of their mother swaying to the beat of an old Temptation song the band was playing. Eric sat next to his wife when his brother got up to meet their mother on the dance floor. Victoria looked at her husband and waited for him to speak. "Dance with me, Vic. Please."

Victoria stood and smoothed the back of her dress, really she was checking for wetness and felt none, well at least not on the outside of her dress.. She walked toward the dance floor and Eric followed. She waited for him to make the next move. He put his arm around her waist and gently pulled him to her, she backed away.

"What's wrong, now?"

"I want you to grip me up like I belong to you." She said barely audible.

"Here?"

"Right now or I'm going to sit back down." Eric sighed and put his arm around her waist again and pulled her a little harder. Victoria shook her head and exhaled but didn't pull away. She put her head on his chest, her arms around his neck and let him lead. She was tired. She knew he loved her, but there was no passion. She hardly felt guilty for running around behind his back, because she needed something that he just refused to give her. Passion, seduction, and just plain ole fucking, were high on her list of what she needed to survive; right along with air, water, and food. She got tired of waiting for him to want her, to *really* want her. Didn't he understand that his wife should be the whore he always wanted? Victoria was fuckstrated. Plain and simple.

"Baby, please tell me what's wrong" He spoke softly. She barely even heard him. She just shook her head and let him sway her slowly in his arms.

"Can I cut in?" Maurice asked when the song changed. "Mama said her feet hurt and she wants to sit down."

Eric looked at Victoria and handed her off to his younger brother, while he returned with his mother to the table.

"You alright, baby?" His mother asked. She was a regal looking woman who looked to be no more than 45 years old. She was almost 65 and proud of her youthful glow. Tonight she wore a beautiful black ball gown with small diamond earrings and a crystal encrusted comb in her up swept hair. "You don't look like a man just awarded a great honor."

Eric looked at his wife, laughing and dancing with Maurice to an upbeat song the band was playing. "I'm fine, mama." He replied as he pulled out the chair for his mother to sit in when they reached the table. His mother followed his gaze and simply said "Mmm hmmm. I see."

To continue reading download a copy of Fuckstrated by Junnita Jackson.

Looking for more to read from Junnita Jackson?
Also Check Out These Titles

If It Don't hurt It Ain't Love
Kat and Dante are scheduled to be married. Will Kat's inability to keep her legs closed keep Dante from saying "I do"? Meanwhile, Tamia's recent visit to the afterlife reunites her with her dead lover James. Will James let her stay with him or send her packing back to reality? Finally, Vatyra lets her guard down enough to let Kevin back in her bed. Will she let him back in her heart; or will his ex-freak-of-the-week forever destroy the meaning of true happiness?

Between My Legs
A Woman Scorned? Not Quite... After playing runaway bride, Kat's world gets turned upside down, yet again. Humiliated and frustrated, Kat, runs straight into the the arms of Karma. A serious force to be reckoned with, Karma, shows Kat the reality behind her love-'em-and-leave-'em ways. Will Karma be enough to help Kat see the light, or will her views on the men in her life be re-enforced?

Fuckstrated
Victoria Manning is married to one of Philadelphia's top administrators in the health care industry. Together they have the perfect "outside looking in" life, with their large homes, invite only social elite gatherings and expensive cars. But sometimes the platinum lining just isn't enough to satisfy her. Victoria craves the attention of a man who

should be strictly off limits. Although, bought up in the same house and raised by the same woman, Eric and Maurice Manning are complete opposites. Victoria's husband Eric is a generous, kind man with a good heart, a good head on his shoulders and wins awards for being the doting husband. Eric's brother Maurice is a lazy corner boy, with a bad attitude and a wicked stroke game. Victoria knows she shouldn't...but sometimes she just can't help herself.

Fuckstrated 2: When one's Not Enough

What do you do when the love of your life loves another? Maurice Manning must face the fact that his growing affection for his sister in law is ruining his life. But with the presence of an old flame and a possible new addition to the family, what seems like the right and mature thing to do will only cause him more pain. Is there really such a thing as love after lust?

Sex Shot Series

What's a *SEX SHOT*? A *SEX SHOT* contains just the right amount of heat you crave. A quickie with just 4,000 to 6,000 words it is sure to get your temperature up! Enjoy a quickie today!

Rope Burn
A mysterious invitation holds the promise of an interesting evening. But who sent the invitation and will they reveal

themselves before the night is through? A mild mannered teacher will get the thrill of a lifetime and will never look at her local bakery quite the same again. Sex Shot Series Short Story

The Librarian
The library is ready to close for the night when a handsome stranger walks in requiring hands on research. Studying at the library has never been this sexy. Sex Shot Series Short Story

Her Wish
There is a time in every girl's life when one must ask an impossible question. Eva's gift to Lux on their anniversary was a night of unbridled passion. Sex Shot Series Short Story

Taste Tester
Annabelle Waters is at college on a full ride scholarship. Her four years of hard work didn't leave much of a social life before college. Now, away from home and jobless, she must learn to take care of herself. An interview at a local company puts more than a few dollars in her pocket. Will Annabelle learn more about biology than her scholarship covers?
About The Author:

Brooklyn born native Junnita Jackson spends her time with either pen in hand or book in hand. Her love of books started at an early age when her mother, who is also an avid reader, gave her two books every payday to read and report on. Pretty soon Junnita's appetite for reading proved to be so voracious her mother gave her a library card.

Shortly after studying Creative Writing at Syracuse University Junnita moved to Central Pennsylvania. She currently works at home on her upcoming writing projects, participates in spoken word events and ferociously loves her family.

Want to connect with Junnita Jackson?
www.Facebook.com/JunnitaJackson
www.Facebook.com/WickedlyErotic
www.Twitter.com/JunnitaJackson
www.JunnitaJackson.com

Join her mailing list here.
http://bit.ly/JunnitaJacksonSignUp